My Dearest Athena

Cowboy Crossing
Book 8

Jessie Gussman

Contents

Acknowledgments

Cover art by Julia Gussman
Editing by Heather Hayden
Narration by Jay Dyess
Author Services by CE Author Assistant

———

Listen to the unabridged audio for FREE performed by Jay Dyess on the Say with Jay channel on YouTube. Get early access to all of Jay's recordings and listen to Jessie's books before they're available to the general public, plus get daily Bible readings by Jay and bonus scenes by becoming a Say with Jay channel member.

Chapter One

The confounded ringing wouldn't stop.

Preston Harding batted groggily in the direction of his head.

Where was he anyway?

A bottle clanked on the floor, falling off the couch on which he was lying—was it his living room? Or someone else's?

He winced at the clanking glass which seemed unnaturally loud.

His head throbbed.

The ringing came again, and he grimaced as pain shot through his skull, pulling at the back of it, tightening the skin of his forehead and neck, before shooting down through his chest and aching in his legs.

He needed a drink.

He needed the restroom.

And he needed that accursed ringing to go away.

He cracked his eyes and the room spun, like it was floating around in space.

He closed his eyes again. This was his house.

The idea that maybe he shouldn't have drunk as much as he had last night probably should have crossed his mind, but it didn't.

He'd been blissfully free from the pain of witnessing his best friend's death for the entire evening, and the physical pain and discomfort he was experiencing now was well worth the cost.

Did he have another bottle in the cupboard?

If not, priority number one for the day was to go get one. Priority number two: drink as much of it as he could before lunchtime.

That would make the afternoon at least bearable.

The pain, more intense and sharper now that he was waking up, shot through him as the ringing began again.

He finally realized it was the doorbell.

Who would be ringing his doorbell?

His best friend Andrew would just walk in.

And...and he couldn't think of another person who would actually want to see him.

Eyes that were so light brown they were almost golden ran through his mind.

She was in town, although for how long he didn't know since she was a hospice nurse, and Mr. Hudson, her last patient, had just passed away.

She wouldn't be coming to see him anyway.

Athena couldn't stand him.

Even if she was his best friend's sister. Andrew would shoot him before he'd let Preston anywhere near his sister in the condition that Preston was currently in.

The ringing started again, and Preston groaned.

It was probably somebody selling something. Why wouldn't they just go away?

His hand reached out and patted along the floor. He couldn't remember if there was anything left in his bottle or not. It had sounded pretty empty when it hit the ground, but maybe his luck would hold, and there'd be a couple swallows to tide him over.

Maybe if he could just get a drink, he could manage to get himself up and at least open the door and yell—in a whisper in respect for his head—at whoever was refusing to go away.

Didn't they know he wasn't answering the door for a reason?

Didn't it ever occur to them that maybe he didn't want to have any visitors?

Preston didn't often get disgusted with himself, but he kinda did at that point.

Shane would be disappointed in him.

Andrew, Shane, and he had been inseparable through their early twenties and done all kinds of dangerous things together. Three cocky daredevils, who thought they were invincible.

Then one day, they all found out they weren't.

That was the day Shane fell off the rock wall they were climbing, ropeless climbing.

They'd listened to his yell echo the whole way to the bottom.

He could hear that yell even now in his head.

He could hear the abrupt way it cut off. Could still feel the pain that swamped over his body, the disbelief.

The shock that ripped between Andrew and him as they looked each other in the eye, knowing that seconds ago, everything was right in the world, and now, just mere heartbeats later, everything was wrong.

He wasn't sure he'd taken a single breath since then without hurting.

The doorbell rang again, and words that he would never have said growing up tumbled off his lips.

Growling deep in his throat, he rolled off the couch rather than even trying to sit up.

Misjudging the edge, he landed on the floor on his stomach with a thump and a few more words that would make his mother cringe.

It wasn't too uncomfortable. Maybe he'd stay here for a while. He put his forehead on the floor, grains of dirt digging into his skin.

He probably owned a broom, but he wasn't sure where it was.

Now there was less time between each ring, like the person standing outside was getting impatient, like they knew he was in here and weren't giving up until he answered. He didn't know who it was, but he supposed Cowboy Crossing was a pretty small town, and even if he didn't know the person at his door, if they'd stopped in town to ask about him, locals would have been able to say exactly where he lived and that he'd be there.

Depending on who they'd talked to, they might have even been told there was no point going out before noon.

And they probably would have heard that they'd have to ring the doorbell until he stumbled to answer it.

Expect to wait a while.

Not everyone in town would say that, but there were a few.

He should feel more remorse about that than he did.

He'd worked hard not to feel anything.

As long as he had enough alcohol, he was successful.

His head felt like it was going to explode. His mouth was dry as a stack of hay in the desert. He really needed the restroom, but he was going to get rid of this person at his door because they'd annoyed him to the point of anger.

He could almost hear his mother saying, *other people don't* make *you angry, you are in charge of your own feelings.*

But he shoved that aside. No one else believed that rubbish, and he wasn't going to either. He could blame the entire rest of the world for his problems.

And he would.

He dragged himself to his feet, leaning heavily on the coffee table before standing with his knees slightly bent and one hand holding his aching head.

Marshaling up all the resolve that he possibly could, he put one unsteady foot in front of the other and made his way to the door, banging his knee on the end table and knocking the lamp to the floor with a sharp clatter that reverberated like gongs through his head.

He didn't give a flip about the light. He never used it anyway. All he cared about was getting rid of whoever was at his door.

He finally made it to the door, fumbling with the lock and jerking the door at least three times before he managed to unlock it and yank it open.

He barely registered that there were two women and a young boy between them before he growled, "What do you want?"

Then his eyes seemed to focus, and he swayed, shock ripping through him.

The one woman looked familiar, but he wasn't focused on her.

Because Athena's golden eyes, filled with disgust and disdain, stared back at him, and he forgot about his headache, his dry mouth, and all of his other problems until he realized how terrible he must look and what she saw.

His eyes narrowed, and black meanness bubbled up inside of him.

She looked down on him, and while she was right and he just couldn't justify himself, she also couldn't possibly understand the pain and the memories.

Chapter Two

Athena's heart beat hard and fast in her chest.

It grieved her to the very depths of her soul to see Preston looking the way he was.

Smelling the way he did.

She wrinkled her nose.

It was a lot easier to hide behind disdainful looks and a disgusted attitude than it was to let him know how seeing him like this made her feel. She wanted to grab him by the scruff of the neck and shake him like a dog, shake some sense into him.

She wanted to hold him, comfort him, and take the pain she knew he felt and carry it for him.

She wanted to take his hand and laugh and make him smile again.

But she couldn't do any of those things.

He'd never noticed her, and the woman standing beside her was proof of that.

"Preston," she said. She allowed snobbery to enter her voice, but she knew she couldn't keep the caring out of her eyes. "Maybe you remember Joyce Oakley?"

He recognized the name. She saw the flickering in his eyes despite the two or three weeks' worth of growth on his face. His unkempt hair hung in his eyes. The wrinkled shirt carried food stains and what she assumed were alcohol spots. Same for the pants he wore, and his socks didn't match.

Not to mention he smelled like an unwashed brewery.

Still, his eyes squinted slightly, and he looked at the woman beside her.

"Joyce?" And then his eyes fell to the boy.

It took about five seconds.

Maybe if he weren't hungover, it would have been faster.

But his eyes widened, and his mouth opened then closed and opened again.

If Athena weren't so irritated with him and with herself for never being able to fall in love with someone else, she might have laughed at that. He looked like a fish.

But it was a serious moment because Joyce claimed that Preston didn't know about Liam.

Watching his reaction, she was positive that Joyce was speaking the truth.

Preston was completely shocked.

But Athena had grown up in Andrew's shadow and had been around Preston from the time he was younger than what Liam was now.

Liam looked like a carbon copy of Preston.

It was obvious Preston saw that immediately.

His eyes shot to Joyce's and then to Athena's.

"What...?" His eyes narrowed, almost like he was blaming Athena for this. "What are you telling me?"

Athena's eyes widened. Why was he blaming her? It was almost like he thought she had brought Joyce here to have a gotcha moment.

"You think you're gonna embarrass and shock me?" he asked with a sneer.

Athena hardened her jaw. "That's not why I'm here."

"Can you make it fast? I have things I wanted to do today."

Athena lifted a brow. "Obviously. Like taking a shower. It must be time for your monthly one."

She sighed inside. Why did she have to be so nasty? Why couldn't she just accept that he wasn't what she wanted and be nice to him anyway? It was the way she treated everyone else.

She didn't look at anyone else and see people who weren't doing what she thought they should, so she was unkind to them.

But even as she was thinking those things to herself, she knew exactly what the problem was.

She cared about Preston.

She knew the potential he had.

He was brilliant. One of those kids that never cracked a book in school and still got straight As. He cut classes, and goofed off, and still aced the tests without a second thought.

And yet, he'd sunk to this.

"Sorry, Princess, that my hygienic habits don't meet with your approval. I'll make sure to check with you before I sneeze."

"That's not your problem. Although it does involve your mouth."

Maybe she should just give up being upset with herself, since everything that came out of her mouth directed at him was censorious.

Maybe that's what he needed. Some tough love.

Or maybe he just needed love.

That was what she wanted to do. She wanted to just not care what state he was in and love him anyway, but she'd seen too many of her girlfriends throw too much of their lives away on men who treated them terribly, used them, cheated on them, and eventually left them, and all the while neglected them. At least two of her college friends married alcoholics.

She kind of thought that was the worst. Because the bottle was their mistress; they didn't need a wife.

She'd seen how they suffered, and she wasn't going there. As much as she wanted to love him anyway.

"Honestly, Athena. This is really none of your business." His eyes shifted down to the boy, and his face changed slightly, although there was still anger there. "You shocked me, which I'm sure was your intention. But if you thought you were going to embarrass me or make me feel bad or guilty, you wasted your time. I can't take care of what I don't know about."

He held Athena's eyes, his own blue and filled with ice.

They used to be gorgeous and filled with laughter and life and the desire to live each day to the absolute fullest possible.

He was so much the opposite of her straightlaced and serious personality. She loved it.

She loved his brilliance. She loved his fun-loving antics. She loved his heart and soul and how he might be a total daredevil and a prankster to boot, but he had soft spots for children and animals, and at one time, she'd thought he had a soft spot for her.

"I'm sorry you feel that way. That's not why I'm here at all."

"I could speak for myself," Joyce said, putting a hand on Athena's arm.

Joyce wore short sleeves, despite the February chill, and Athena had no trouble seeing where Preston's name was tattooed on her arm.

There was a line through it, and "Brian" was tattooed below it. There was a line through Brian as well, with no other name taking its place.

Athena hadn't thought it was any of her business to ask if Joyce had decided that tattooing her current flame's name on her arm was not a good idea, or whether she hadn't had a current flame after Brian.

Not that it mattered.

Liam was what mattered to her the most.

But Joyce was her patient.

"Then do so." Preston shifted, still holding the door in one hand, and put a hand on the doorframe. "I don't have all day."

Athena managed to not snort over that, but she wanted to.

She also wanted to call him out and point out that all he had to do all day was find himself more alcohol and get drunk.

Which was obviously all he'd been doing every day for a long time.

He was living off his parents' money, another thing that he'd had such an advantage—he could have been anything with his brains and his parents' wealth and his affable and friendly personality.

He could have done anything, been anything, gone anywhere.

And yet look at him. The only thing different between him and a homeless bum was that he had a home.

Thanks to his parents.

Preston probably looked worse than a bum right now.

His situation was assuredly worse, because he'd thrown away so much.

Joyce obviously was having trouble trying to figure out where to start. Athena allowed her time to think.

There were reasons why Joyce never told Preston about Liam, and there were reasons now why she was.

They were her reasons, whether or not Athena felt they were legitimate. It didn't matter.

The snake tattooed around Joyce's neck moved as she swallowed.

"Liam, would you go sit in the car, please?" she finally said, as though realizing this might not go the way she wanted it to, and she didn't want her son to get hurt.

"Can I play games on my iPad?"

"Of course." Joyce put a hand on her son's shoulder.

Athena said, "Would you like me to go with him?"

"No. Please stay. You said you would."

That was the whole reason Athena was here. She hadn't wanted to be a part of this. Except she kind of was.

"Why don't you come on out here and sit on the porch, if you're not going to invite us inside," Athena suggested to Preston, pleased that she was able to keep her voice modulated and almost kind. When she wanted to sound frustrated and angry and, yeah, hurt.

Because if Preston had loved her, he wouldn't have allowed himself to be like this, not if he felt she was worth living for, instead of turning his back on everything and basically waiting to die.

Preston didn't say anything but sighed, like he was put out, which he probably was. He stepped out, spreading his hand around. "You can see there are no chairs. But you're welcome to sit on the floor if you want." He kinda sneered.

Joyce lifted her chin while Athena ignored him. She waited for Joyce to sit down before she sat on the step next to Joyce.

Preston closed the door and walked over, leaning his shoulder against the porch post. "I take it the boy's mine."

Athena's throat tightened.

Obviously, he'd had a relationship with Joyce, a more-than-friends relationship, considering she had his name tattooed on her arm and they had a child together.

Athena had only found out a week ago, and she'd mostly gotten used to it, but it still hurt.

Not that it mattered now. But if it was true that there was a fine line between love and hate, she wished she knew where that line was so she chould cross it. She felt like it would be easier if she hated him.

"He is." Joyce lifted a shoulder that wasn't exceptionally thin.

A person couldn't tell by looking at her that she'd be dead in three months. Or less.

"And there's a reason you've kept that from me. A reason you're telling me now."

Maybe they should have been questions, but they weren't.

"There is," Joyce said, almost defensively. Athena felt bad for her. This was a difficult conversation to have, and Preston wasn't making it any easier.

"So am I to find out about it anytime today?"

"How about you just relax. You could, oh, I don't know, try to be a little bit nice?" Athena couldn't keep her mouth from moving.

Preston didn't used to be a jerk. He didn't used to be a sloppy drunk. He didn't used to be any of the things he was now.

Maybe she was just in love with memories. Except she kinda felt like once you loved someone, you didn't just quit. Not if it was true love, which took work and time and effort, except she'd never had to work to love Preston.

She'd always had to work to hide her feelings.

"I didn't tell you about Liam because, as I'm sure you can figure out, your family has a ton of money, and your mom has a lot of influence. She would have tried to take him, even if you didn't want to."

Preston's eyes lowered, and he looked away.

A cat, pretty white with tabby orange spots on it, came around the corner of the brown flowerbeds.

Athena hadn't spent too much time around his parents. It was her understanding that Preston didn't spend too much time around them either, for the reasons that Joyce just mentioned.

They had money, and they weren't afraid to use it to try to get their way.

"All right. I'll give you that," Preston said grudgingly. "Why now?"

"Because I've been diagnosed with an inoperable brain tumor, and the doctor has given me three months. But he said that was probably a generous estimate."

Preston reacted about the same way Athena had.

His eyes got huge, and he looked at Joyce, really looked at her. "Three months?"

She nodded.

When she told Athena, she'd cried.

She seemed to be coming to grips with the reality of her life because her eyes were dry.

She had lost weight, although she still didn't look sick, but she needed high doses of painkillers most of the time for the headaches, and her balance had been getting worse almost on a daily basis. Joyce had told Athena the doctors said her tumor was fast-growing and aggressive.

"I know. You can't see it. But I'm not going to starve to death because of the tumor. It's just gonna take me a little every day. I'll be surprised if I'm walking next month this time."

The doctor had said her motor functions would go, and in the papers that Athena had read, it said that possibly her ability to swallow would be affected.

The growth of the tumor was documented. The areas it would attack next were not.

Preston might be hungover, and he might have a pounding headache, if the lines between his brows were any indication, but he definitely wasn't slow.

"You want me to get to know the boy."

"Yes," Joyce said. "And I want you take him. He's yours. I raised him up until this point. You're going to have to take over from here."

"Whoa. Whoa, whoa." Preston put his hands up and straightened off the post that he'd been leaning on. "Does this look like the kind of man you want raising your son?" He pointed his fingers up and down his body.

Athena could answer that question.

No.

That was absolutely not the kind of man she wanted raising her son. She wanted the old Preston.

Actually, she didn't need crystal-pure Preston.

She just wanted Preston who wasn't intent on drinking himself to death. Who stopped focusing on himself and was once again able to look at the world and see people he could help, challenges he could face, and mountains he could climb.

The cat had made it up the steps, and it weaved in and out of Athena's legs.

Athena reached down and petted it. Someone was feeding it because it looked healthy and sleek.

It wasn't afraid of her and pushed into her hand. Its throat vibrated in a soft purr. Looking at Preston now, a body would have trouble believing that he might be an animal person, but knowing him like she had back before the accident with Shane, she was pretty sure this cat was probably his.

Maybe there was hope for him after all.

"You're the father. Why wouldn't you take him?" Joyce's tone was accusatory. "Are you denying that he's yours?"

"I... I... This is... You have to know this is a huge surprise. I'm not exactly set up to be a father."

"Well, you have three months. At the most." Joyce glanced over at Athena, and her eyes seemed to plead with Athena to take it from here.

Athena allowed herself to sigh inside, but she didn't allow her dismay to show on her face.

She didn't want to be the one to say what else needed to be said. But she would.

The cat stepped into her lap.

Athena rubbed its ears absently.

Then she took it in her arms and stood. If she were going to be assertive and take control of the situation, she couldn't do it sitting down.

"That's not all. But that's part of the reason why we have several suggestions. You don't know Liam, and he doesn't know you. And he doesn't have much time to get to know you before you're going to be his sole guardian. And yes, your name is on the birth certificate."

Preston's eyes widened, like he hadn't even considered that. But then he looked away, his arms crossed over his chest, his shoulder once again leaning against the post. Athena stroked the cat in her arms. It snuggled down and purred against her chest.

"All right, Sergeant Princess, give it to me with both barrels."

Athena's eyes flickered. Sergeant Princess was what he always called her when they were teens. The way he said it brought back flickers of the old Preston.

Hope had flared up in her chest, but she snuffed it out. Nicole, her girlfriend who was married to an alcoholic, was constantly going from hope to hope to hope only to have them dashed.

She didn't want to fall into that trap.

"Because you need to get to know Liam and because our time is limited, I propose that Joyce move in with you. Obviously, you know I'm a hospice nurse, and she's also hired me to be a personal caregiver. I'm working in conjunction with my agency, and I'll be her main nurse during the day. There will be at least two others, but it will be mostly me." She wanted to be clear, because having his home invaded by an army of people would be less appealing than mostly her. She thought.

"No," Preston said, without even moving. He certainly didn't look at her. "Not doing it."

"We figured that's what you would say. But consider the implications. Joyce's house is two hours away, and that's where Liam will be, unless we make this change. Because, obviously, with the limited amount of time that she has left, Joyce wants to spend as much of it with Liam as she can."

"I'm not asking you to marry me," Joyce said quietly. "I'm not asking you to have a relationship with me at all. I don't want that. I don't even want to be here. But when Athena suggested this, I knew she was right."

Athena wanted to close her eyes. She hadn't wanted Preston to know this was her idea.

His head turned, and his eyes looked at her with interest. Bloodshot as they were. "You suggested this?"

"Doesn't it make sense? Liam needs to get to know his father. Joyce's willing. And she's too far away."

That square jaw—the one she'd dreamed about all through high school—set, and a muscle in it twitched as he looked out over the driveway toward where Joyce's car, an older model that needed a paint job, sat.

Maybe he was remembering that Joyce didn't really have a family. She never knew her dad, from what she'd told Athena, and her mom flitted from job to man to job to man and was currently with a man in California as far as Joyce knew.

Joyce had said they'd kind of been hippies growing up, and Joyce had never put down roots or known any of her other family or even, in most cases, if she had a family.

It was a little late to start looking for them.

"Joyce can stay at her house. I can come visit. Weekends. Or a day or two each week."

"Saying that you actually do that," Athena said and managed to not add, *which I doubt*, although she really wanted to, "you do realize that if Joyce lives the entire three months that she's been given, that's only thirteen times? That's if you come every weekend or once a week. And that's if she makes it that long."

Joyce had faced her death and accepted it, but still Athena hated to talk about it and rub it in, so to speak. If it were her, she wasn't sure she'd want it put so bluntly.

It seemed necessary since Preston, unsurprisingly, was being unreasonable.

"The doctor told her it probably wouldn't be long, maybe not even a month. She probably won't be walking this time next month. She might not be breathing either. That's four times that you'll have seen Liam. Is that what you want for your son? To be left with a man that he's seen four times before he loses his mother?"

The cat in her arms felt Athena's agitation and twisted.

Athena set it down and watched as it walked over and wove between Preston's legs. She stared at the mismatched socks, one of which had a hole in the heel, and the jeans which were frayed at the bottoms. They were covered in food stains and what looked like stains of something being spilled on them. She looked away.

Sickened.

So much potential. So much waste.

Chapter Three

Preston didn't see a way out.

The last—very last—thing in the world he wanted was a child to be responsible for.

But he wasn't so far gone that he didn't know he couldn't just walk away from his responsibility.

No matter the legal implications of his name being on the birth certificate. That was the least of his concerns.

He didn't need a paternity test to know that Liam was his.

It had only taken one look, maybe five seconds, and the facts were right in front of him.

That and Joyce and he had done everything they needed to do in order to produce a child.

For months.

The relationship hadn't been long, but apparently, that didn't matter.

As all those things ran through his mind, over and over, as Joyce and Athena talked, slowly, eventually, he started to get used to the idea that the kid was his.

Started to wonder about his life. The things he'd missed and the things that he might have been able to provide for the boy, if he'd been around.

Who was he kidding? He couldn't even take care of himself. What would he have provided for a child?

Joyce had been before the accident, and he certainly hadn't been serious about her.

To his shame.

Joyce had the same coloring as Athena. Her eyes weren't quite as golden, they were just brown, but her hair had been the same color, and she'd been about the same height.

Their personalities were completely different, and that probably contributed to the brevity of their relationship.

Even back then, he'd been a jerk.

He hadn't been thinking about long-term relationships, or children, or anything remotely associated with responsibility.

No wonder Athena never looked twice at him.

She'd been so serious.

So driven. So bossy.

He had liked it. He needed someone who wasn't afraid to boss him a little and give him structure.

But not someone like his mother, who passed the line from bossy into controlling.

Athena was very much like his mom, commanding and sure, a take charge kind of woman, but she differed from his mother because she had compassion and a kind, caring soul that saw what no one else could.

At one point, he thought she saw good in him.

Not anymore.

Because there was nothing good to see.

He blew out a breath and ran a hand through his hair. Way too long. He needed it cut. If he was going to be an example to his son, he needed to get cleaned up.

Shane had been raised by a single mom. He'd always joked about being jealous of Andrew's and Preston's two-parent families and of Preston's family's wealth.

Liam's life so far could have been exactly like Shane's life.

He couldn't think of his friend without pain surging through him.

Taking responsibility for his son wasn't a choice to be made. He was going to do it.

And in doing so, he could somehow honor Shane by making sure that another child didn't have a life where he never knew his dad and grew up with his poor single mother.

"Try not to get a big head about it, Sergeant Princess, but I think you're right." He waited to see if Athena would gloat.

She didn't.

He hadn't thought she would. That wasn't the kind of person she was.

Athena did exchange a glance with Joyce. He felt like a heel, because when Joyce looked back over at him, she had tears in her eyes.

He'd been a jerk. He'd pretty much been a jerk his entire life.

Had a son. He had a real live son.

He didn't want that boy, the child that carried his genes, to grow up to be a jerk. He wanted him to be someone who contributed good things to society.

He wanted his son to be everything he had never been.

Sure, maybe his son would be brave, a daredevil, a risk-taker, but he should also be kind, compassionate, willing to give up his rights, his time, his resources to help other people. To be a blessing. To reach out and cheer someone up.

His eyes crawled on their hands and knees over to Athena, who was leaning toward Joyce, looking straight ahead as Joyce whispered in her ear. Her face was serious, but she nodded.

And as far as he knew, Athena didn't know Joyce, hadn't known her until she'd been assigned to be her caretaker.

She wasn't being paid for today most likely, and she definitely wasn't getting paid to be treated as badly as he treated her.

When Athena had a patient, she put her entire heart and soul into that patient and their family.

He remembered seeing her at Mr. Hudson's funeral standing with Mrs. Hudson beside the casket. Athena was a rock.

No one paid her to do that. It was just what Athena did.

When he said he wanted his son to be kind and compassionate and a blessing to others, he didn't want his son to be like him.

He wanted his son to be like Athena.

Chapter Four

The bell jingled as Athena walked into the feed store in Cowboy Crossing.

Because of taking care of Mr. Hudson for the last months of his life, she'd gotten to know the Hudson family fairly well.

Marlowe Hudson, who was married to Clark Hudson, smiled at her from behind the counter when she walked in.

"Athena! It's great to see you. I thought you might be leaving Cowboy Crossing now that...your assignment is up." Marlowe's face dimmed slightly, and Athena couldn't blame her for stumbling and not wanting to mention Mr. Hudson.

It had been a blow to the family, as deaths always were, especially since this had been mostly unexpected and rather quick.

"I'm actually going to stay in town a little longer. My new assignment is from out of town, and you wouldn't know her. However, I know you know Preston, since he was around here growing up and moved here not long ago."

"Of course. I don't see him in here much, but he was good friends with Andrew and Shane." Again, Marlowe stumbled over mentioning the friend who had died while rock climbing with his friends.

He hadn't been from Cowboy Crossing either, but the three friends had spent time in town.

Marlowe's face brightened again. "Perfect timing for you to come. Ivory is here," she said, referring to Chandler Hudson's wife. "She's back looking at the garden seed. This time of year, everybody's ready to get their hands back in the dirt." Marlowe held her own hands up. "I'm not even a gardener, and I can't wait to get out and plant a few things."

"You garden," Athena said. "You eat stuff that you grow."

"True. But around here, there are *serious* gardeners, and that's not me."

"Yeah, me either." She'd chosen to be a nurse, and she loved it. But the older she got, the more she knew she'd love to have a family to care for more than patients. It just wasn't something the Lord had given her. It wasn't something her heart had allowed, stuck as it was on someone who could never love her back. Not like he loved the bottle.

"I guess Clark has the children?" Athena asked.

"He does. We've actually hired someone to work behind the counter here, but it's going to be another week before they can start."

"Spring's a busy season."

"It sure is. And Clark wants to be in the field. I can't blame him. I know his mom will watch the children, but we didn't want to overwhelm her with her still grieving." Marlowe shook her head. "These are her golden years. She was supposed to be able to enjoy relaxing and not working so hard and maybe doing some traveling with her husband." Marlowe's lip turned back. "I hate to see her spend the rest of her life alone."

Having been with the Hudson family, especially Mrs. Hudson, for several months while Mr. Hudson declined, Athena knew that Mrs. Hudson was highly unlikely to be spending the rest of her life alone. There had been a man who had been very attentive to her, although not disrespectful or inappropriate in any way.

However, Athena was pretty sure that man was interested in more than just a platonic relationship with Mrs. Hudson.

That probably wasn't her information to hand out.

"What makes you think that Mrs. Hudson's never going to get married again?" Ivory came up and said, taking the words right out of Athena's mouth. Although she probably wouldn't have said it quite like that. While she was good friends with Marlowe and Ivory, she wasn't part of the family and didn't feel quite that relaxed.

Marlowe's mouth dropped open like she had never even considered the idea. "Well... Well." She had to laugh. "I suppose it's possible. I hadn't considered that. Mrs. Hudson is just, you know, married to Mr. Hudson. There's no one else."

"I know what you mean," Ivory said with a sweet smile, her face glowing. Being married to her movie star husband had been very good for her. She'd come out of her shell and blossomed beautifully, like a tender rose, sweet and pretty, on the end of a hearty climbing bush. "I suppose you've been in the family longer than I have, but still, seeing her in town, it's hard to picture her with anyone else. But Mrs. Hudson isn't that old. I mean, maybe to us, but she's barely fifty. I'm sure she would love to do all those things that you said, and I'm sure she would love a romance to go with them."

"Mrs. Hudson's a beautiful woman. On the inside as well as the out. She deserves to have a man who can appreciate that and to enjoy many more decades of love and romance," Athena said.

That wasn't giving anything away. But maybe it was opening Marlowe's eyes, which in turn would hopefully help the idea to make its way to Clark and the rest of his brothers. The boys were going to be shocked otherwise when Mrs. Hudson introduced them to her new love. Which Athena figured was probably inevitable, although not soon, since Mr. Hudson hadn't been gone long.

"Speaking of romance," Ivory said, her eyes sparkling. "You're still available and looking, correct?"

"I suppose you could say available. I'm not looking." Athena ran her fingers over the edge of the counter, although she tried to keep her words firm and confident. They were true. She wasn't looking. She'd already found someone.

"I think Athena has her eye on the guy she wants," Marlowe said with a sly smile.

Athena's eyes widened, and they shot to Marlowe. Had she figured it out?

"Don't look so surprised. You've always made googly eyes at Preston. But honestly, after what happened to him and the way he's handled it, it's probably a good thing he's never noticed you."

Well, that kinda shot a pang through her. Marlowe just said matter-of-factly that he never noticed her.

Lovely.

Just what a girl wanted to hear.

Truth hurt. But it was better to have the truth and be hurt by it than to have stars in her eyes and believe lies.

"Well, you're definitely right that he's not ready for a girl. That's for sure."

"I happen to notice that you didn't deny you've had your eye on Preston for quite some time," Ivory said, looking somehow sweet and serious.

"I can't," Athena said simply. "I would prefer he not know it though. I'm pretty sure he might not hate me, but he definitely doesn't like me much."

"I wouldn't be too sure about that," Marlowe said, somewhat secretively. "You know Clark and he are pretty good friends. He's been to a few of the single dads' meetings in town. I believe your name has come up more than once."

That definitely sounded like interest, but she wasn't going to question it. She didn't want to look interested, even if she was.

"That's a dead end for me. I think I've been stuck on him so long it's almost a habit. A bad habit. I'd like to break it, because I really would like to have a husband and family but not someone who loves his bottle more than his wife."

"I have to say you're smart for that," Ivory said, her eyes sad. "I don't even know if my mom knows for sure who my dad is, but I believe that we can place most of the blame for the fact that she doesn't know on that very reason. He liked the bottle more than he loved his family."

Athena moved, putting her arm around Ivory in a side hug. She'd been blessed to grow up in a home where there was both a mother and a father, even if her parents had been somewhat absent as they got older. She hurt for Ivory, who obviously missed the love of her father.

She'd heard other people say different things about how it affected them, such as they weren't sure their parents truly loved them because one or the other had walked out of the family, or had left the family for a new love, or just never gave them any time or attention.

All of it was harmful and hurtful.

All good reasons why she could never be with Preston.

Even if he quit, could she trust him not to go back?

She'd never even entertained that idea, because she had never gotten that far. It didn't enter her thinking, since he hadn't quit. There was no point in worrying any further.

Ivory had slipped her arm around Athena's waist and squeezed as well.

"I'm so glad I have another assignment in Cowboy Crossing. It's difficult to go to a place where you know no one and then be faced every day with the immanency of death..."

"And to do it alone, with no friends there to support you," Marlowe finished for her, coming around the counter and embracing them both. After a moment, Marlowe leaned back a little and tilted her head. "There are all those jokes about group hugs, but you really do need them. You need to know that you have that comfort and that support that you can turn to when you have trouble facing life on your own."

Ivory nodded. "God gives us friends for a reason. He knows we need that physical touch as well as just the idea that there's someone standing behind you, supporting you."

"Isn't that what a marriage is for?" Athena asked, just a little teasing, because both Ivory and Marlowe had great marriages.

"Of course. But there's a difference between marriage friendship and friendship friendship. You need both."

The bell rang, and they squeezed once more before breaking apart, Marlowe going around behind the counter and Ivory putting her things down to check out.

Athena was kinda stuck on what Marlowe said about "needing" the marriage relationship. She felt like it was a need.

Maybe she should give up on Preston and actively search for someone else. Although honestly, she'd spent enough time away from Preston that if she were truly going to get over him, she probably should have already.

She waved goodbye to Ivory, nodded at Marlowe, and wandered down the aisle of the store, looking for the boots she'd come in for.

She wasn't sure exactly whether she was sold on the idea of there being a soulmate for each person and if a person didn't find their soulmate, then there was no point in getting married.

She was pretty sure that wasn't true. Pretty sure that married love was less about the tingles and excitement of finding the exact right one and more about simple determination, perseverance, and commitment to keeping one's word, even when it was hard.

It also had to be about loving your spouse and children and doing what was best for them. Someone with an alcohol addiction couldn't possibly even begin to be able to keep a commitment like that.

That meant, as much as her heart might not want to hear it, Preston was not available.

Chapter Five

Preston stood back against the wall and watched as two burly dudes expertly guided a hospital bed into his living room and put it in the spot Athena had cleared for it just thirty minutes ago.

She had cleared the spot, cleaned it, and muttered under her breath about slovenly people and men who do not clean up after themselves, and he thought he heard the words "disgusting pig" and "alcoholic," although he could have been wrong, but at that point, he'd gone out to the back porch and sat down on the narrow step, holding his head in his hands and wishing he had a different life.

Wishing hadn't made it so, and when he lifted his head, nothing had changed.

He wasn't nearly done wishing when he'd heard the truck pull in and figured he'd better go offer to lend a hand if necessary.

It wasn't. The men knew what they were doing and were adept.

Much more adept than he would have been.

Athena didn't even need to stand and micromanage anything.

He wasn't being fair.

She wasn't as bossy or commanding or micromanaging as he chose to imagine her in his head.

She was just organized and driven and quite capable of getting things done, no matter what was standing in her way. If she couldn't go through whatever obstacle was in her path, she found a way around it or over it or under it.

He just always tried to see her in the worst light possible.

Mostly because making her look worse made him look better.

Deep down, he knew he'd never be good enough for her.

He stood with his arms crossed over his chest, and he was sure the look on his face was glowering, at the very least.

Unsurprisingly, he had a headache, and honestly, he wasn't quite sure he was ready for the chaos that was about to descend on his household.

More than that, he wasn't quite sure he was ready to be a father.

The men were almost finished, and Preston couldn't stand the idea of being left alone with Athena. So he pushed off from the wall and walked to the door.

"Where are you going?" Athena looked up, and maybe she didn't mean for her words to come out sharp and quick, but that's the way he heard them.

"So you're moving Joyce in, and now I have to check with you before I walk out my front door?" he said. His tone wasn't exactly kind.

Yeah, his words made her eyes widen, and he regretted them.

But they were out, had already shot to her ears and her heart, and he couldn't take them back, so he didn't even try. Just waited with his hand on the doorknob, conscious of the men whose heads had picked up at his tone and words and whose hands had slowed before they busied themselves again and tried to ignore his rudeness.

"Of course not," she said, with a look that said she didn't expect anything better out of him.

"I'm glad I can live up to your low expectations." The words were out, and he hadn't meant to say those either. Athena seemed to loosen his tongue in all the wrong places.

Definitely time for him to go.

He opened the door and walked out.

Cowboy Crossing wasn't huge, but it did have a barbershop, and he stopped there first before he went to the feed store. He didn't really have anything he needed to buy, just wanted to kill time to keep from going home.

He'd been meaning to pick up a pair of gloves and figured he could at least do that.

Something to occupy himself to keep from having to go back to his house and all the things he had to face there.

Clark Hudson's wife Marlowe was behind the counter, and he nodded at her as he walked in. He spent some time just looking at the shelves, staring at them without really seeing anything, and wondering if he was up for all the changes that were going to be happening in his life. That were happening now.

He didn't want to lose his peaceful home.

He didn't want people there who would see what he was doing and judge him for it.

He didn't want to have to change what he was doing because of those people.

He didn't want to have to be responsible. A dad. Didn't want to be nice, to engage in conversation, to brush shoulders with people constantly.

It wasn't even the idea that death would be in his house. He'd seen death. He'd seen death in the worst way possible.

He lived with the memory of that terrible death every day.

Not a day had gone by that he hadn't heard Shane's yell falling away until it stopped abruptly.

The alcohol could mute his mind. But he could hardly drink himself into oblivion and pass out on his couch when he had a woman who was dying beside him while her caretaker looked at him with scorn and derision.

Maybe he should rent a place until things calmed down. Until he was ready.

Would he ever be ready?

He paid for the gloves without doing more than grunting at Marlowe's smile and cheerful comments about the weather, then he stepped out onto the sidewalk, wondering if there was something else he could do to kill a little time.

He hadn't figured anything out when he saw Deacon Hudson stepping out of the church and closing the door behind him before walking down the front steps.

Deacon was a great guy. Preston had spent time with him at the single dads' group meetings that he'd gone to over the years. It was where the men of Cowboy Crossing hung out, not necessarily for just single dads. He really liked Deacon, having a lot of respect for him, his life, and the wisdom he occasionally shared.

But he was the last, very last, person Preston wanted to see right now.

He didn't want anyone telling him how ridiculously pathetic he was and how he needed to grow up and take responsibility and face the things that life had thrown at him with a lot more dignity and responsibility than he had been showing so far.

Unfortunately, after glancing up and down the street, he realized there was no place where he could duck into, unless he turned around and ran right back into the feed store, and knowing his luck, Deacon was on his way to the feed store. It seemed to be the place where folks in Cowboy Crossing went on a daily basis.

His dilemma was moot when Deacon saw him.

Deacon's face broke into a grin, his hand lifted, and he called, "Preston! Wait up. I wanted to talk to you."

Preston hadn't been moving, so he didn't need to stop. But he didn't walk to meet Deacon like he might have another time.

They shook hands. With Deacon smiling and looking so happy to see him, it was hard for Preston to keep his black cloud around him.

Being happy always felt like a betrayal of Shane.

"I've heard there's some changes happening at your house," Deacon said.

"I guess," Preston replied, not wanting to talk about it.

"Well, I won't press because it's really none of my business. But I was wondering if you'd give me a hand. I have some feed I need to load in my pickup which is sitting behind the feed store already. If you'd help me out, I'd appreciate it."

Relieved that he wasn't going to have to have a heart-to-heart or even a surface conversation with Deacon, Preston almost smiled. "I'd love to."

"That's a lot of enthusiasm for tossing fifty-pound sacks around. I wasn't expecting that."

Preston grunted. "I thought I was going to have to talk about Joyce and death and Athena taking over my house. Tossing feed sacks around sounds much better."

"Can't say I disagree."

"That's odd coming from a preacher. You talk about those kinds of things all the time."

"That's true. But that doesn't make it easy. Of course, life is pretty much about not doing the easy thing," Deacon said, sounding casual and not even looking at Preston as they kept walking. It couldn't have been a rebuke, but it hit Preston like it was.

Or maybe that was just his conscience hitting him. After all, drinking himself into oblivion every night was much easier than facing the painful memories. He'd been doing "easy" for years.

"Life is actually about trying to do the easy thing. Sometimes, it just doesn't work out," Preston said.

Deacon's step hesitated slightly as Preston's words drifted off in the late January breeze. "We'll just have to disagree on that. The easy thing is what we usually do because that's our default, right? The easy thing? But normally, that's not the *right* thing to do."

They'd reached his truck where it was backed into the dock. A half a skid of horse feed sat at the edge of the cement.

"You want to jump up and hand them down to me, and I'll stack them on the pickup?" Deacon asked.

"That's gonna be a big load for your little truck."

"I know. But I'm just taking it to Loyal's farm, which isn't far. But yeah, she'll be overloaded."

"I know how she feels," Preston muttered, feeling like the truck with too much feed on it was his life with too many people and too much responsibility and too many changes at one time. Overloaded.

"I'm listening if you want talk about it," Deacon said, jumping into the bed of the truck as Preston climbed onto the dock.

Preston didn't say anything. He really didn't want talk about it. But Deacon hadn't even been giving advice on purpose, and he'd already given him more than enough to think about.

Not choosing to do the easy thing.

Of course, he knew that was usually right. Sure he did.

But no one actually lived that way.

Except...some people probably did. Resisting what was easiest in favor of what was right.

Maybe, he wouldn't have said anything. In fact, he probably would never have said a word.

Except, he was a father now.

Crazy.

He could hardly believe it, and while he still hadn't quite gotten used to the idea, he did want to be a good influence in his son's life. He wanted to be able to teach his son good things. Like how to get over death.

How could he teach his son that when he hadn't figured it out himself?

He picked up a sack, turned and carried it the few steps to the edge of the dock, then handed it to Deacon.

"I want to be a good influence on my son. But I'm not sure how to start. And honestly, everything that's coming down makes me want to move out of my own house."

There. He didn't like admitting things that were hard, but he'd already said he was overwhelmed. Maybe Deacon would have a few good words for him.

They stacked five more sacks of feed before Deacon finally answered.

"I guess you probably know you really can't be a good father if you can't stay sober."

Yeah. He knew.

"I haven't had anything to drink since I found out. It's been a rough week. Alcohol numbs the memory of my friend's death."

Deacon didn't say anything more until he set the feed sack down in the bed of the truck, aligning it and slapping the top to make it lie flat. "Did it ever occur to you that you could be thankful for that death?"

"Thankful?" Anger stirred in Preston's chest. Obviously, Deacon knew nothing. "How can I be thankful that one second, my friend was there, and the next, he fell into eternity, screaming, until the screaming stopped. That's supposed to make me thankful?"

Deacon shrugged, but his face was tombstone serious. "It's all in your perspective. You could spend the rest of your life suffering for his death. Or you can look at it, decide what you want to learn from it, and think over the lesson."

Deacon's words were so foreign to anything Preston had ever considered regarding Shane's death that he froze, not even noticing Deacon had his arms out for the feed sack that Preston held.

Learn a lesson? What kind of lesson could he learn, other than no more rock climbing without ropes?

He'd learned that.

No more daredevil stunts.

No more thinking he was invincible.

He slowly lowered his feed sack into Deacon's arms. "What lesson do you think I should learn?"

Would it be something that would help him be a better father?

"I think that's probably up to you." Deacon grunted as he set the sack down, adjusted it, and slapped the curve flat. He straightened and looked over at Preston. "Isn't it?"

"What do you mean? I learned it hurts. I learned it sucks. I learned I don't ever want to go through that again."

"Do you think those are the right lessons?" Deacon asked, coming over to the edge of the truck and putting his hands on his hips.

"I can't imagine what other lessons there would be."

Deacon lifted his shoulder. "Look around, especially at nature, and death is natural, and there are lessons everywhere. God planned it that way. I think sometimes in our modern life, we've gone so far away from nature, and we got away from the lessons it teaches. What seems like common sense and naturally right becomes a stunning revelation when we spend most of our time in artificial environments playing and working on man-made things."

Preston turned, slower than he had been moving, because he was thinking. He picked up a feed sack, but his mind was twisting Deacon's words in his head. "I guess I'm still not sure what you're saying."

Lessons? He supposed he could see nature teaching about reaping and sowing. That was pretty obvious. It was a true lesson. True in his life, true in nature. But anything else? He couldn't say.

Deacon slapped the feed sack down on the others and walked back over before he answered. "Well, I suppose if I were a government official, I could look at that death, and I could say I learned that people are stupid, too stupid to think for themselves, and we need to make laws. Laws that say you can't climb walls without ropes or maybe pass a law that will bar access to that area and not allow people there at all."

Preston grunted. "That's right on. Not what I think should happen, but definitely the way some people think."

"I know. I personally don't feel that's the right lesson to learn, but it is a lesson that some people might take from that." He lifted his hat and scratched his head before settling it back down. "We want to legislate and regulate everything until all people are doing is sitting around and looking at each other and breathing, but not on each other because we don't want anybody to catch anything, because that's all it's safe to do. I don't think that's the way life's meant to be lived."

"Me either." Certainly not. He'd done a lot of dangerous things in his time. Some of the things he'd done were illegal, some of them were legal at the time but had since been regulated. He didn't believe in that either. What was the point of being free if all you could do was sit and stare at your TV set?

"When that happens, other people are robbed of the opportunity to learn as well. And don't take me wrong, I don't think people need to die in order for people to learn lessons, but when something like that happens, you can either look at it as a terrible tragedy and mourn and feel guilty and sick and sad and blame yourself or whatever, or you can look at it as God being in control. He allowed it to happen. Then ask, 'what does he expect out of me because of that?'"

"I see."

He believed in God. Of course. Maybe, though, he believed in God because it was just easier to believe in God than it was to believe that something came from nothing. It was just too unreasonable that, instead of decaying like the natural order of things would dictate, whatever the something was that came from nothing grew and formed itself over millions and millions of years into a man.

Talk about unbelievable.

Definitely God was easier.

But easier wasn't always better. Deacon had just said.

Belief in God was easy.

Faith in God was a completely different story.

And that's what Deacon had been saying. That he had to have faith that God would work everything out...for good.

The verse came to his mind, the one from his childhood, where God works everything out for his good. He couldn't remember the exact words, but the lesson was there. That's what it was that Deacon was saying.

"In order for God to work that out for my good, I have to learn the lesson he wanted me to learn."

"That's right. God can do it anyway, but our lives become better as we become better. Wiser. More accepting of the things we can't change, and more willing to admit that maybe we don't know as much as we thought we did."

All that was true, but he still didn't understand what lesson God might have for him.

He figured...why not? Why not ask?

After all, he was just as likely to come to the wrong conclusion as the right one himself.

He knew he hadn't been handling Shane's death well.

But he had never even dreamed of thinking about being thankful for it.

He could see, easily, that it was better to look at it and see how he could learn from it. How he could make his own life better. Wasn't that a better legacy for Shane than wallowing in alcohol?

Shane would say so.

He'd known it. Of course, he'd known it. But maybe he just needed to have it framed in the right way in order for him to be inspired to take the first step.

Or maybe it was because he knew his life was going be changing, and he wasn't going to have any choices about taking any steps. So he wanted to take the right ones.

He waited for Deacon to slap the bag down and walk back over before he said, "I don't disagree with anything that you're saying. In fact, it makes a lot of sense. So much sense that I feel like I should have thought of it myself, although I hadn't been thinking anything of the kind." He hooked a thumb in his belt loop and wrapped the other around his neck. "But I just want to say that while I agree with what you're saying, I'd rather you tell me what to do. Just say, 'This is what you need to do.' Because your theory makes sense, but I don't know how to apply that."

It wasn't the best explanation he'd ever had, but he didn't know how to say it. Basically, he just needed to know what to do. He didn't have to understand. He just wanted to do the very best for Liam that he could.

Deacon grunted, and the smile on his face irritated Preston just a little. He'd been serious. And Deacon was laughing?

"I'm not laughing at you. I'm laughing at myself. I say that to God all the time. Just tell me what to do. Don't give me this book full of archaic words and tell me somehow I'm supposed to figure out principles and abstract ideas and somehow use it for everything from raising my kids to knowing who to vote for to having a romantic relationship with my wife."

Deacon grunted again, and Preston found himself smiling. It did seem kind of crazy that one book would contain all of that.

"But, you know, the same principles pretty much apply to everything. Sure, they don't tell me that if my wife's been up all night with the baby, she'd appreciate me cooking supper and doing the dishes, and it doesn't tell me that my kids need me to take them fishing, and it doesn't tell me which politician is lying the least." They both chuckled. "But the principles are still the same. And the biggest one, beyond loving God—because that's what makes you want to be a better person, right?—is treating other people how you want to be treated. It's simple."

"So that's how I raise my son?" It seemed like raising a kid would be a little harder than that.

"To start. It's a start. With kids, I've found the best thing you can do for them is to be who you want them to be, because they're gonna look at you and imitate you anyway. It's just the way kids are."

Preston nodded. He remembered following his dad around and putting his feet in his dad's footsteps, imitating his dad's hand motions. He found himself saying things his dad said, and probably his facial expressions were similar as well. He wasn't exactly like his dad, but he saw how Liam would probably imitate him.

Right now, his life was most certainly not worth imitating.

Deacon opened his mouth, then paused, like he was seriously

reconsidering whether or not he was going to talk. "I don't like to give people advice they didn't ask for, but I just want to say that I think you have an opportunity to not just be a father to Liam but to give him a home and parents who love him."

"Parents?" he asked, surprised.

Deacon stared straight into his eyes, and Preston thought that he might be saying more than what his words actually said. "Parents."

Preston nodded, his brows lowered, his eyes on the rearview mirror of the pickup. Parents. That was plural. Deacon thought that he had the opportunity to...give Liam a mom too?

Deacon shifted, putting a foot up on the tailgate of the truck and leaning an elbow down on his knee. "I'm not saying you should do anything for the sole reason of making sure that Liam has a mother that he needs. I am, however, saying it's possible. I don't want to be the one to tell you what lessons you're supposed to learn, but one I can see that might be applicable would be don't miss the opportunities that you've been given. Because you never know when you won't have another one. And you don't want to waste a lot of time on regrets."

Preston wasn't sure he understood that completely, but Deacon had given him a lot to chew on. He picked up the last bag of feed, and Deacon lowered his foot, taking it from him and dropping it down with the rest.

"Thanks for your help, man."

"Thanks for the advice."

"Hope it was worth something for you."

"I'm sure it will be." If nothing else, Deacon had given him a slightly different way to look at the world, a much better way than he had been. Now, if he could just do something about it.

Chapter Six

Athena scooped the eggs out of the skillet and onto the plate on the counter.

After setting the skillet down, she placed a slice of cheese over the top of the eggs and carried the plate to the table.

"Did you get your homework done last night?" she asked Liam who was sitting at the table playing a game on his phone.

He made a grunting sound that could have been yes, no, or a statement about taking a shuttle to the moon. Impossible to interpret.

"Was that a yes?" Athena asked, her brows raised and one hand on her hip.

The kid looked up at her. "You're not my mother."

Athena blinked, and while her teeth wanted to clench, her heart wanted to cry. "I know. But I'm going to give a report to your mother, and I'd like to be able to tell her that you did your homework." She lifted her brows. "Did you?"

"All except my math which I didn't understand."

"You didn't understand it? Was it different than what the teacher explained in the class?"

"I didn't understand it when she explained it in class."

"Was there no time for questions?"

"I'm not gonna ask a question. I'd look stupid." Liam gave her a look like she was slightly more intelligent than a roach and went back to the game on his phone.

"Math is not my favorite subject, but tonight when you get home from school, I'll stay, and we can go over your math at the kitchen table before I leave."

"I can do it."

Athena's head jerked up. Preston stood in the doorway, the look on his face slightly uncertain and completely at odds with the confidence behind his words.

Athena tried to keep her brows down and her eyes natural, but they both wanted to extend off her face. She wasn't sure she wasn't letting them.

"Why would I want you to help me?" Liam said belligerently and without looking up.

"Because someone needs to. Can't go through life without knowing how to do math."

"I know how to do math. This stuff with shapes and circles is stupid. There's no need for it."

Athena swallowed, considering her next words. She kind of enjoyed her psychology class in college and had noticed that reverse psychology often worked.

As rebellious as Liam seemed, and she was cognizant that might be because of the changes in his life—going to a new school couldn't be easy and having his mother lie dying in the other room couldn't be a walk in the park either—but since he seemed determined to disagree with everyone, she might be able to get him to disagree with her and take Preston's side.

Hopefully, Preston didn't get too upset with her.

She took a breath. Then she straightened, trying not to cringe when Liam grabbed his spoon and concentrated on shoveling eggs into his mouth while holding his phone and continuing to play his game with one hand.

"I'm sorry, Preston, I don't think you're probably the best person to help him with his homework."

They'd been here a week, and this was the first morning that Preston had come downstairs before Liam left for school.

At least he'd been sober every day.

Athena had been leaving around six o'clock, so she didn't know what he did in the evening, but apparently if he was drinking, it wasn't so much as to have him be hungover in the morning.

Still, she really wanted to encourage this, him getting down before Liam left for school, but she wanted to take this other gamble, because it might pay off bigger in the long run.

Still, the shock on his face almost made her rethink her decision. Betrayal sat there, too.

"I'm his dad. Why would I not be the best person to help him with his homework?" He lowered his brow and grunted. "You think I should be throwing this all on Joyce? She can barely take care of herself. Breathing is difficult for her."

Three days after they moved the hospital bed in, Joyce had woken up unable to get out of bed.

Apparently, Rusty—Joyce had named the tumor after an old boyfriend whom she hated—had decided to take her ability to walk first.

"I'm just saying that because everything was so easy for you in school. I don't think you ever studied. Do you really think you'd know how to help someone who doesn't know how to do it?"

Watching out of her peripheral vision, Athena could see that Liam had kinda slowed in his gameplaying and was listening.

Good.

It was her backhanded way of informing the kid that his father was brilliant.

Hopefully, the kid had enough sense to realize that those genes ran in him, too.

Also, unless she missed her guess, it would give him a newfound respect for his dad, who he didn't know too much about as far as Athena knew.

Now the kid at least knew his dad was brilliant.

Hopefully, that would affect the way he thought about him.

"So you're saying because I never struggled, I'm not qualified to help people who do?"

Athena lifted her shoulder. "That's reasonable. You don't understand what he's going through."

"But I understand how to do math. That's what matters here, isn't it?"

Athena opened her mouth, but Liam interrupted her. "He's right. He doesn't have to be perfect or whatever. All he has to do in order to help me is know how to do it. He doesn't have to have all those other girly feelings you're talking about."

Athena did not allow her lips to twitch at all. And there was no smile in her eyes.

She stepped back, putting her hands in the air. "Okay. Fine. If you'd rather have him help you, just say so."

"I'd rather have him help me. Not you."

His words hurt her heart, and she wasn't having to hide a smile anymore. She had to hide the fact that she wanted to flinch and, maybe in some small way, retaliate.

It was probably a natural thing, when someone hurt you, to want to hurt them back. Even if it was a kid.

Regardless, he had a lot of anger and resentment, probably because of the unfairness of life taking his mother away. She swallowed that hurt, bearing it. Burying it.

It might have been a little bit of hesitation that crossed Preston's face, but she wasn't sure.

She went back to the stove, slipping more eggs on a plate and carefully placing another slice of cheese on them. She grabbed the orange juice she'd poured earlier and the silverware and walked toward the doorway where Preston stood.

"Excuse me, please," she said without looking at him. "The rest of the eggs on the stove are yours if you want them."

"I don't believe it's your job to cook breakfast for everyone, is it?"

"No, but if I'm cooking, I might as well cook for everyone." She looked up at him, steeling herself because his eyes always did something to her. "Is that a problem?"

"No. I appreciate it. But I don't think you should have to do more than what you're paid for."

"I believe you should always do more than what you're paid for. It's just a good way to live."

He nodded slowly, his mouth open slightly as though he were thinking about what she said, or maybe he was thinking something else.

She was done trying to figure him out, done wasting time on him. She was not going to spend her life pining after someone who cared so little about himself and the people around him that he would waste his life drinking himself to death.

He moved, and she pushed by without saying anything more.

Walking into the living room, Athena set the plate of eggs and the juice on the coffee table and adjusted Joyce's hospital bed to a sitting position.

When she'd gotten there this morning, she'd helped Joyce with her morning toiletries and helped her brush her hair and put on something nice.

Preston was no boyfriend, but Joyce was a woman and Athena knew she'd want to look as good as she could. Joyce might be dying, but she still seemed to admire Preston.

Maybe women were just attracted, in a kind of idiotic way, toward unapproachable men who were obviously going to neglect and treat them badly.

There was small comfort in the fact that she was not the only woman in the world who was attracted to such a man.

"I heard you fighting with Liam about his homework."

Athena wouldn't have termed that a fight, exactly.

"I just want you to know I raised him better than that." Joyce lifted her arm and fingered the piercings that went from the lobe of her ear clear up around and through the top cartilage. There must have been ten or twelve of them. Athena hadn't taken the time to count. "Just because I lived a little wilder life than you did doesn't mean I didn't try to make my son learn some manners."

"I know. We all just do the best we can. Sometimes, it turns out that our best is good enough, and sometimes, it turns out it's not." Athena fluffed a pillow and put it behind Joyce's back. She stood back. "Is that comfortable?"

"No one can do it like you can."

Athena laughed. "I've just been doing it longer. Lara is new and hasn't learned the secret technique of fluffing pillows."

Joyce smiled. "You're the only one that can make me smile, too."

"Maybe I'm the only one that tries."

"That too. Same."

"If you tell me that I cook the best eggs, I'll feel like I need to win the nurse of the year award."

"I can't say for sure. Nobody else makes me eggs."

"Are you up to feeding yourself this morning?" Athena asked.

"I think so." Her lips turned down though, and Athena figured she was wondering just how much longer she'd actually be able to do it.

Part of her inability to walk wasn't necessarily that she couldn't move her feet, it was just that she couldn't get her balance. Couldn't keep it.

Same problem with her hands. She could pick the egg up, she just couldn't always guide her hand to her mouth.

"Unless you don't want to clean up the mess. Then you'd better feed me."

"I don't mind cleaning up messes. It's my job."

"It's not your job to make sure that my kid did his homework. But I'm glad you did."

"Did you hear Preston say that he was going to help him

tonight?" Athena couldn't keep a little of the excitement out of her voice. Liam needed his dad now more than ever. It was the only family he had. She couldn't help but be excited that Preston seemed to be stepping up.

"We've been here a week. It's the first time he's come down before Liam left for school. I'm not holding my breath that he's actually going to be here after school or that he's going to actually help Liam with his homework."

"Well, I'm glad you're not holding your breath at least. I don't want to have to do the whole mouth-to-mouth thing. Not this morning anyway. I had onions on my eggs."

"If I stop breathing, just let me go," Joyce said with a bit of a sly smile. "I don't want mouth-to-mouth with onion breath."

Athena pulled the chair close to the bed and sat down, picking up the plate and the fork and feeding Joyce.

She hadn't even considered that Preston wouldn't do what he said he was going to. Could Joyce be right?

She dismissed that thought immediately.

In all the years that she'd known Preston, he might have been an alcoholic, he might have been a daredevil, and he might have been inclined to take the easy way out, but he'd never been dishonest. And he'd never not done what he said he was going to do.

Joyce would see. Athena would bet on it.

Chapter Seven

After Athena walked by him, swirling the air and somehow making it smell like rich chocolate and coffee, even though she was holding eggs and cheese, Preston shook his head and walked to the stove.

This was the first morning since he'd quit drinking more than a week ago that he actually felt like eating.

Yesterday had been the first day he thought he was probably going to live.

Before that...he might have gone back to the bottle if he'd had any in the house. Deacon and Andrew had come over. He thought someone else might have been there too. And Athena had checked on him. Of course.

Not that she'd said anything. But he remembered her several times.

She'd asked the man he didn't know if Preston was going to live.

The man had grunted and said, "He's too stubborn to die."

Athena hadn't looked happy with him, but Preston had closed his eyes, unable to keep them open any longer. His heart had felt like it was going to beat out of his chest, and his hands had been slimy with sweat. He felt sicker than he could ever remember feeling and if he'd have died, it would have felt like a blessing.

But something about Athena's look had made him think that maybe she didn't want him to. Maybe he'd try to live, just to see if he might be right about that look.

He scooped out the rest of the eggs and threw four slices of cheese on them. A smaller skillet held what looked like cooked onions and mushrooms, and he dumped that on top of it.

Today, he actually felt...hungry. Starved, in fact.

He took his plate and went over and sat down at the table with Liam.

"It was nice of you to back me up there, Liam."

Liam looked up, a little bit of a smile in his eyes, a little bit of pride, and a lot of wariness. "You must really be my dad, since you let us move into your house."

He hadn't really talked to the kid, even though he'd been home in the evenings. He hadn't wanted to push too hard to begin with, and he had to admit having the whole hospital bed in his living room took a little getting used to.

"You can't tell me that you look in the mirror and see your eyes, and then you look at mine, and you can't tell that they're the same?" Preston said, squeezing ketchup over the mess on his plate.

"Lots of people have blue eyes. Ours aren't the only ones in the world."

"You're right. I guess they're just the same color and, more than the color, the same shape."

"If you say so." Liam shrugged.

"You don't have to take my word for it. Don't you want me to be your dad?" He said it kind of casually, because he hadn't realized until the words were out that he actually did care.

It wasn't essential that Liam accept him, ever, let alone today, but he shouldn't have said words that he knew could hurt him if the answer wasn't what he wanted.

He thought he could handle it.

"I don't care. Most of my life, I thought Dad, I mean Rusty, was my dad. But then Mom came home and found him buck naked in the shower with some blonde chick who was also buck naked, and she decided he wasn't my dad anymore." Almost as though he knew his words were shocking coming from someone as young as he was, Liam lifted challenging eyes to Preston. "She can kick you out the same way?"

Preston breathed in and out. Who was he to try to teach morality to anyone?

He hadn't been married to Joyce when they'd conceived Liam.

Marrying her hadn't even been on his mind.

In fact, at that point in his life, he had pretty much pushed everything he'd learned in Sunday school as far back into the nether reaches of his conscience as he could. He didn't want to feel guilty for what he was doing. Who did?

He wanted to be able to do whatever he wanted, whenever he wanted, and he didn't want to have some religious mumbo jumbo making him feel like he should feel guilty.

He totally bought into that.

The older he got, and the longer he lived, the less he felt like it was mumbo jumbo.

After all, if he'd listened to it and not been with Joyce, there wouldn't be a little boy sitting in front of him, accusations in his eyes and in his words, and hurt echoing through all the recesses of the kitchen and humming in Preston's ears and down his nerve endings to his own heart.

Which ached.

He wouldn't be confused about who his dad was, wouldn't have been lied to, wouldn't wonder why his real dad hadn't been there for him all his life.

If Preston had listened to that mumbo jumbo, it would have saved his son a truckload of pain and hurt.

"I hope not." He couldn't give an answer that wasn't honest. "But

I guess if you stay here for any length of time, you're gonna find out pretty quick that I'm not perfect."

Liam snorted. He finished the last of his eggs and pushed the plate away. "I didn't think you were," he mumbled.

"Good. And I don't think you are." He looked at Liam's plate. "You can take that to the sink."

Liam gave him a look but didn't argue, and when he pushed his chair back, he picked his plate up.

"Just because we know we're never going to be perfect doesn't mean that we shouldn't try to be the best that we can be." He wanted to add that in order to be the best he could be, he needed the Lord's help, but he didn't want to overload Liam with too much.

"I think I'm pretty good the way I am," Liam said, almost as a challenge. "But I can see a lot of room for improvement for you."

Preston paused in the act of putting eggs in his mouth.

He almost laughed. The nerve of the little kid.

"If you're here when I get home," Liam emphasized the if, "I'll have my math, and I'll let you help me. But only because Mom will be mad if I get an F."

"Well, that's a good reason," Preston said, talking with his mouth full and immediately wishing he hadn't.

As far as he could tell, that was one bad habit that Liam didn't have, and he didn't really want him picking it up from him.

"Have a good day at school."

Liam grunted as he left the room.

Preston finished his eggs and carried his plate to the sink. He no sooner set it down than Athena bustled into the kitchen.

"Would you mind sitting with Joyce for a few minutes while I clean up in here?"

"I can. You don't have to clean up. I can get it."

"I made a mess. I don't mind getting it, but she asked for you, and I thought I would give you some privacy."

Preston was pretty sure that hospice care, and even the personal nursing she'd mentioned, didn't include all the things that Athena did. But he liked what she'd said. That she always wanted to give someone more than their money's worth. He liked the idea of living like that.

Maybe not even giving people more than their money's worth but giving them more than they expect.

That was one of those ideas that were sweet to think about but hard to live.

When he did things the easy way, he definitely wasn't giving people more than they expected. In fact, he caused everyone around him to lower their expectations of what he would do.

He didn't want to be living up to the lowest common denominator. After talking to Deacon, after thinking about Shane, if he really wanted to learn lessons from that, one of them could be *always give more.*

That chocolate coffee smell stirred around in his brain, but he didn't say anything more to Athena before he walked out.

He still, after a week, couldn't walk into his living room with confident steps.

Instead, he always kind of paused at the door, peeked in, and then walked as though his feet were bare and the floor was sprinkled with glass shards.

Silly, he knew, but he just felt uneasy and uncomfortable.

"I'm not gonna bite. You can come closer," Joyce said, her voice raspy.

"I wasn't too concerned about that, but thanks for the reassurance," he said, stepping over to the side of the bed and perching on the edge of the chair. "Athena said you wanted to talk to me?"

Joyce nodded, and he noticed there was a bit of egg left on her lip.

He wasn't sure what to do about it, so he tried to ignore it.

"Athena hates your guts," Joyce said in a conversational tone and so casually that Preston jerked back just a fraction of an inch before he said, "What?"

"She hates you." Joyce's voice lowered. "As in, she can't stand you and wishes you weren't here. I think you should avoid her as much as possible to keep from upsetting her."

Preston wouldn't argue with Joyce, and he'd kinda figured for a while that Athena looked down on him, thought he was a loser and no good, and basically disliked him. However, he supposed hearing it from someone else hurt his feelings in a way he wasn't expecting.

Not to mention, it wasn't that long ago Deacon was hinting that he and Athena would make a good couple. Make good parents for Liam. And he didn't think Deacon would recommend that if he didn't think that Athena was capable of, if not loving him, at least liking him enough to marry him. At some point. Not tomorrow. But at some point.

"Well. I kinda suspected that. But thanks for telling me." He kinda wondered why she felt the need to. But he supposed he didn't need to ask. "Is that what you wanted to tell me?"

"Are you gonna tell me how much you hate her and what a wicked witch she is?" Joyce's face did not look happy.

"No." He wouldn't do any such thing. Because it wasn't true.

Joyce's face scrunched up, and while she probably wasn't the most beautiful woman that Preston had ever seen, the way it twisted now made her look downright ugly. Not in the physical sense, just from the nastiness that seemed to be coming from her. It surprised him.

He didn't remember her being like that.

"Don't you know that when someone hates you, you're supposed to hate them back?"

Preston nodded, leaning his elbows on his knees, steepling his fingers together. Joyce wasn't going to be with them much longer, and he didn't see any point in lying to her. Not that he would have anyway.

"I guess I know that. But I guess there's just no way I could ever hate Athena. Maybe she does hate me. Mostly because she's right, and I don't want to admit it. Not because there's anything wrong with her." He turned his head and looked at Joyce.

His words, far from reassuring her, had brought tears to her eyes.

"You can go now. I don't want to talk anymore."

He sat there, stunned. That was weird. One second, she was dishing, the next, she was dismissing him.

After about five seconds, she closed her eyes and turned her head away. He straightened from the chair and stood by her bed.

"If I can do anything for you, let me know."

"Fine," she said, the word clipped.

It all seemed very strange, but Preston couldn't quite put his finger on what was going on. He figured it didn't matter anyway.

He'd never been able to figure the female brain out, certainly hadn't had any great insights in the last week. He probably never would.

Chapter Eight

Preston was ready when Liam got off the bus that afternoon. Athena was ready too.

After Liam had greeted his mother and chatted with her a little, he'd walked with Preston into the kitchen, where Athena had a tray with crackers and cheese, meat, and apple slices already sitting on the table and ready for them.

Preston stopped in the doorway, looking at the table, before his eyes went to Athena, who was standing at the counter with her back toward him, chopping up potatoes for supper.

"Looks like you have some afterschool snacks, Liam," Preston said. But his mind was whirling. It wasn't part of her job to make snacks for him and his son.

It wasn't part of her job to make supper.

It hadn't been part of her job to ask about homework this morning, or he wouldn't even be here with his son, getting ready to sit down to work on math.

Do more than expected.

He'd scoffed at that as being unreasonable, something that no one ever lived up to.

Athena wasn't just anyone.

But it also highlighted the fact that she was light-years ahead of him, and he could work the rest of his life and still never catch up.

Still, Deacon seemed to think there was a chance. Although he hadn't exactly said. Despite what Joyce said, which, when he'd thought about it, he'd decided that maybe it was her tumor talking, he'd be a fool not to try for even a small chance.

He almost opened his mouth and told Liam to thank Athena for the snack tray, and then he remembered what Deacon had said about setting an example.

"Thank you for taking the time to make a snack tray for us, Miss Athena." He almost stumbled over the "Miss," but again, he needed to be the example, not just say what to do.

Liam's eyes were on him when he looked down, so he jerked his head a little and lifted his brows.

Liam got the hint, and he smiled like Preston and he were conspiring together behind Athena's back. Conspiring for good, as they shared a grin and Liam said, "Thanks, Miss Athena. I'm hungry. Am I allowed to eat it?"

She looked over her shoulder, her hand stilling.

"Hello to you, too." Then she grinned a little. "I guess I should have known that the food on the table would be the first thing you guys would notice. And, Liam, you can have as much of it as your dad will allow you, but although I won't be here, supper should be ready at six. Did you have a good day at school?"

"I guess," Liam said, walking forward and dumping his book bag on the chair. He reached for a cracker, and Preston said, "Better wash your hands first, kid."

He almost thought Liam was going to ignore him, because it took another second for his hand to stop. But it did, and Liam turned and went to the sink.

Preston had done a lot of thinking today while he had been out at Loyal's ranch helping him install a computer-controlled monitoring system for the maternity stalls in his horse barn.

That was the type of business his father was in, and he'd helped and worked in his dad's business until the accident.

His parents called him periodically. His mom wanted to know how he was, and although he knew she did it out of love, he felt like she tried to micromanage his life as well.

He avoided her.

But his dad had asked multiple times each year when he was coming back to the business.

His parents had enabled him long enough.

It was time he started pulling his weight.

Or, like Athena, pulling more than his weight. Maybe it was a weird thing to wonder, but he couldn't help but think that the world would be a completely different place if everyone were like Athena, doing more than expected.

He followed Liam over to the sink and waited while Liam finished washing his hands.

The chocolate and coffee scent that he associated with Athena shimmered in the air, and he breathed it in.

"How was your day?" he asked.

Athena made three more slices with the knife before she stopped abruptly and jerked her head over to look at him.

There was not much space between them, and he could see the shock in her eyes as she said, "Are you talking to me?"

He made a show of looking around the kitchen, and then his eyes rested on her once more. "You're the only person in here, other than Liam, and we've already figured out that his school day was good."

"Well, I think you want to get a little more than 'good' out of him, but if that's an acceptable answer, my day was good too. Thanks for asking."

He supposed he never really thought about women in terms of types or kinds, but he supposed there were ladies whose personalities were like curves, circles and ovals, sweet and soft and round.

But Athena was sharp. Her wit quick. Her eyes picking out

everything. Her mind processing it and making snap decisions, and she acted on them without wavering. Matter-of-factly.

He liked her sense of humor. And he liked the way her mind worked.

Her eyes crinkled, and the corners of her mouth quirked when she saw him smiling.

"So how about you show us how we get something more than 'good' out of you about your day."

A little of her smile dimmed, and her eyes went to Liam who turned the water off and was drying his hands.

"I love my patient, and I got to have several nice conversations with her. I also got to read one of my favorite books aloud to my patient who had never heard it, and she enjoyed it as much as I did. And while I made you guys a snack tray, I helped myself to a little bit of it, and so I had good food today, too. Nobody died. Nobody went to the hospital. It was a good day." She lifted her brows and gave Preston a challenging look. "How was your day?" she asked, with not a little sarcasm.

"It was good," he said with one side of his mouth quirked up before he turned to the sink and turned the water on.

Athena snorted and went back to chopping her potatoes.

Preston grinned to himself as he finished washing his hands. Then, while he was drying them, he leaned a hip against the sink facing Athena.

Liam happily munched at the table, so he figured it wasn't like they needed to be in a huge rush to get started on his math work.

"Yesterday when Deacon was in town, he told me that his brother Loyal was installing an electronic monitoring system for the maternity stalls in his horse barn."

Her head swiveled to him. "That's the kind of business that your dad's in, isn't it?"

"Do you want to hear about my day, or do you want to ask me twenty questions?"

His eyes twinkled at her, and he was gratified when she grinned, ducking her head, and said, "Go on."

She understood he was goofing with her.

Some women would have gotten offended at that and wouldn't have understood that he was just picking on her from the conversation they'd been having.

It was always nice to be with someone who understood you.

Of course, he thought unexpectedly, that went both ways.

He needed to understand her and not just be happy about the fact that she understood him.

The snacks on the table were probably for Liam, but maybe she knew he'd be hungry too.

She knew there needed to be supper, so she did it. Whether or not she was doing it for him, since her patient would be eating too, he couldn't say for sure, but still, he appreciated it.

How did that happen? How did someone become a person who knew what other people wanted and had it ready for them so that it was there when they thought about it?

Definitely not a question he'd ever thought about before.

"So I went out there today and did some measuring, did some figuring, and, after I talked to Loyal about it, placed an order for the things that I'll need, which should be here the day after tomorrow. In the meantime, Madeline, his wife, ordered takeout for lunch, because she can't cook."

Athena laughed. "I think she can make bologna sandwiches. At least, once when she came to visit Mr. Hudson, she and I sat in the kitchen for a little bit, and she made her kids bologna sandwiches, anyway. They ate them and they didn't die, so I thought that maybe she's learned a little bit since she got married."

"Yeah, that's pretty amazing. I think they're leaving in a few weeks to go tape another episode of their cooking show. Loyal is looking for someone to do his spring field work, since production got pushed back because of some scheduling conflicts with the studio. They were supposed to be filming it in January."

"You know Madeline is one of the only people I know who has a personality that could pull off having a world-famous cooking show, lines of cookbooks, and a whole empire built on food, when a bologna sandwich is the best she can do in the kitchen."

"I guess we all have our talents."

Athena scraped the potatoes off the board and into a pan on the stove and nodded without looking at him.

He wanted to know what she was thinking, why that comment would have made her go quiet. But he figured it was more than time for him to get started on this math stuff.

He turned toward the table, where Liam was happily squeezing two crackers together over cheese and meat that was at least two inches thick as he opened his mouth and tried to fit the entire cracker tower in it in one bite.

"If you ever had any doubts about that kid being yours, watching him do that should reassure you," Athena said, her voice coming from behind his shoulder.

"You said that like I do that every day."

"If I hadn't said something, I guarantee you two minutes from now, you'd be doing the exact same thing, only your cracker pile would be twice as big, and you'd probably have instigated a competition with Liam as to who could fit the tallest sandwich in their mouth."

"You spent way too much time with your brother and me growing up."

"I know. And Shane wasn't any better."

He froze.

Her eyes looked at him steadily, almost a challenge in them, as though she knew talking about Shane was his weakness. And she hit it on purpose.

But, knowing Athena, and watching her now, she hadn't done it on purpose to hurt him, she'd done it on purpose to show him that it was okay to talk about him.

One part of him resented that. He was an adult. He could decide when he was ready to talk about Shane again, when he wanted to start healing, when he wanted to put Shane's name out in the air like that.

But part of him knew it'd been long enough. More than long enough.

"You're right. Shane would have been an instigator, pushing us to do more and go further." His words weren't as confident. In fact, they were rather low and almost meant for the two of them. Like he couldn't say it louder. But even talking about him was a step in the right direction. More than he'd done at any point before.

"Well, don't let me stop you. But maybe you can remember that you are supposed to get some math done." She looked around his shoulder. "Liam, maybe you can make sure this big oaf actually helps you with your math and does more than have eating contests with you, okay?"

Liam smirked. "I'll give him five minutes to eat, then he needs to start doing math whether he likes it or not," he said, eyeballing Preston in a rather exaggerated kind of way, but that was better than the sullen belligerence he'd shown this morning.

Preston wanted to turn and put his arms around Athena right then. She'd gotten a smirk out of the kid. And he seemed almost happy. Of course, food had a tendency to do that to boys, and maybe Athena knew that. Probably she did. She'd spent enough time around him and Andrew and Shane over the years.

Whatever they did, food was always involved. Even if it was freeze-dried and vacuum-packed, meant to go with them up a mountain.

He wanted to mouth a "thank you" to her, but she wasn't looking at him, so he just turned, thinking that he'd thank her later. And maybe do a little more talking as well.

Chapter Nine

"There's mashed potatoes and mushroom gravy for supper," Athena said as she held Joyce's hand, bending over her bed, "and I also made an egg custard if you don't feel quite up to the heartier stuff." She gave her hand a squeeze, still amazed it didn't feel thin or small or even weak really, but Joyce was dying nonetheless. "Okay?"

Joyce rolled her head and opened her eyes, squinting a bit before she seemed to get her bearings.

"The room's spinning." She closed her eyes again. "I know it's just me, but I feel dizzy when I have my eyes open."

"Then keep them shut. It's okay," Athena said soothingly.

"I want you to fluff my pillows before you go. No one does it like you do."

Thankful that Joyce had said that softly so that Kevin, the nurse who was spending the evening with Joyce, didn't hear her, Athena didn't say anything but adjusted the top pillow and then carefully arranged her shoulders before doing the other two.

"Is that good?"

"Yeah. Who's your replacement?"

"Kevin."

The hand that had been gripping hers tightened. "Don't leave me here with him. He hates me."

For a woman who was dying, her grip was surprisingly strong.

"I can speak to a supervisor tomorrow, and I can have Kevin reassigned." Even though her voice was pitched low, she saw movement out of her peripheral vision in the doorway. She lifted her eyes. Thankfully, it was Preston.

She nodded and lifted her brows, hoping that he got her message and kept Kevin in the kitchen where he was putting his lunch in the refrigerator until she was done speaking with Joyce.

Not that this didn't happen all the time. Especially with patients with brain injuries and tumors. Their personality shifted and changed sometimes for no reason at all. They said things that weren't true, things that they would never say if their brain wasn't being taken over by an intruder.

Athena was tempted to pat her hand and say, "I think this is Rusty talking," but Joyce wouldn't know it, and as a nurse, she was required to report any patient complaints.

It was just as likely that after she left, Joyce would complain to Kevin about her.

Again, this was something their supervisors knew and made allowances for.

"Can't you report him now? Can't you get me someone else?" Joyce's voice held fear, and her grip was cutting off circulation in Athena's fingers.

"If you'd like me to stay, I can."

"Don't leave me." Joyce's other hand came up, and now Athena's fingers were clutched between both of her hands.

"I won't. I'll stay." She tugged a little on her hands. "Let me go to the kitchen, and I'll talk to Kevin. Maybe I can switch a shift with him until things get straightened out tomorrow. Okay?"

"You're not gonna leave?"

"I promise. I won't leave."

Joyce's face relaxed, and her eyes closed. A smile touched her lips. Satisfaction and peace replaced the fear and anxiety of just seconds before.

"I need my hand," Athena said. While Joyce's fingers had relaxed, they hadn't completely let go.

"Come right back."

"I will. Maybe Liam will come out and talk to you for a bit."

Her eyes glanced up, where Preston's back disappeared from the doorway. She assumed he'd probably gone into the den to get Liam from where he was watching TV.

Joyce's fingers loosened, and Athena shrugged out of her coat and hung it back up on the hook where she had gotten it from and walked into the kitchen, pulling her phone out of her pocket.

When she had been staying with Mr. Hudson before he passed away, Mrs. Hudson had been kind enough to offer her a room in their home. Mrs. Hudson had extended that offer after his death and then again after she found out that Athena would continue working in Cowboy Crossing.

Athena had taken her up on the offer. She always had her schedule laid out for Mrs. Hudson, and she wanted to text her and let her know that she wasn't going to be home if Kevin agreed to the switch.

This wasn't the first time she had to talk to someone who a patient was upset with or didn't want to have, but the conversations were never easy.

She didn't look forward to it.

"Hey, Kevin," she said as she walked in the kitchen.

He stood up from the refrigerator and closed the door with a snap. "I thought you were leaving?"

They'd already gone over the paperwork and the information that he needed to know, and Joyce's medication schedule and all of the other things were on the iPad in the room.

If Athena hadn't stopped to tuck Joyce in and say goodbye to her, she'd have been out the door and on her way home now.

Her back hurt, and so did her feet. She was ready to sit down.

But once supper was over, the evening shift wasn't usually difficult at all. Especially now, in the early stages of Joyce's decline.

"Well, you know we're dealing with a brain tumor patient."

Kevin's eyes went from curious to irritated.

Athena shrugged her shoulders, and her lip pulled back. She lifted her hands, like this wasn't her doing. "I'm sorry."

"Man. What's she saying?" His voice wasn't exactly unkind, but he sounded frustrated.

"She wants me to stay. She says you're mean to her. I know it's not true. You and I worked together with Mr. Hudson, and he loved you. But with a brain tumor..."

"I know." Kevin closed his eyes. "It just reeks because I just bought a house. I need the money from my shift."

"If it's any consolation, I'll talk to Catherine tomorrow and tell her that you've always been a perfect nurse. But she knows that, of course. And she's familiar with brain patients as well."

"I know. This is just life. Still, it's frustrating," Kevin said, turning and yanking open the refrigerator door before pulling out his lunch and closing it. "You're good here?"

"I am. Sorry."

"You're going to talk to Catherine and let her know?"

"I will." Typically, their supervisors were pretty relaxed and allowed them to move their shifts as necessary, as long as they kept track of it on the private webpage designed for that purpose. "I'll log in and make sure everything shows up. I'll put her comments in and my own comments about brain patients."

"Thanks."

Kevin left without saying anything more, and Athena gave herself a few minutes to wilt into a chair and put her arms on the table, laying her head down on top of them.

She needed to make some phone calls, needed to get her iPad out and make those changes as well. She just needed a couple minutes.

She'd also been planning to help decorate for Andrew's surprise birthday party with Reagan. She would have to call her and let her know that she wouldn't be able to make it this evening. Hopefully, Reagan could reschedule for tomorrow.

Pushing up, she took a deep breath and went to get started.

Chapter Ten

Preston finished off the water in his cup and set it beside the sink.

Liam had actually done a really great job on his math. Once Preston had shown him how to do it, a slightly different way than what the teacher had shown him, everything had clicked in his head, and Liam did his work as fast as he could move his pencil.

Preston hadn't expected the sense of pride that filled his chest as he watched his boy, biting his lip and scrunching his face up until the light dawned and the thoughts in his head fell into place and brought a smile to his face as the work became something he could do, instead of something he struggled with.

He hadn't known what to expect when he'd said he'd help his kid with his math. He just knew that was what parents did, so that was what he needed to step up and be, but it had been...maybe not fun exactly but...gratifying.

He still didn't feel qualified to be a father, hadn't really adjusted to that in his head, but he thought he might be getting there.

Padding across the kitchen, he looked out the doorway, expecting to see Athena stretched out on the couch. She'd been getting her stuff ready when he'd walked through going to the kitchen to get a last drink and turn the lights out before going to bed.

Since he quit drinking, this was the time of night where he got the most restless, and not exactly longing for the bottle, but an irritation that he just couldn't reach to soothe, like an inside itch that couldn't be scratched, and he ended up walking around, checking things, even eating something.

He supposed it would go away, and he was more blessed than most people. Some just couldn't give it up.

But if he was going to do right by his son, he didn't have a choice. He had to get things pulled together.

Maybe too, he was putting off going to bed.

When his head touched the pillow, that's when the screaming started. It ended, abruptly, just like it had when Shane fell off.

Then it started again, with the same abrupt ending every time. Over and over and over again.

Joyce's eyes were open, so he walked over to her. "You doing okay?" he asked softly. Not knowing what else to say. She'd just been a fling for him. He hadn't had any deep emotions attached to her. And still didn't.

Other than maybe shame and regret.

He'd been a stupid idiot when he was younger, he'd done a lot of dumb things, and he'd hurt good people.

Joyce was one of those people.

"Fine as I can expect to be, I guess," she said, her voice sounding sleepy and a little weak. Or maybe it was his imagination.

"Where's Athena?" It was the question he'd wanted to ask first, but he felt like he should at least inquire after her health before he demanded to know who her nurse was.

"I told you she hates you."

"I know. Do you know where she is?" Even though he'd heard some of what Athena had said about brain patients and them not knowing what they say sometimes, it still shot pain up through his rib cage and out his backbone to hear Joyce say that Athena hated him.

He didn't want it to be true.

"She said she was going outside and taking a short walk. She said she'd be gone for ten minutes, but she'd be close."

"Thanks." He started to turn, then he stopped. "Can I get you anything?"

"I'm fine."

"Okay."

He grabbed his coat and opened the door, walking through, closing it behind him.

He didn't really have anything he wanted to say to Athena. Well...he had lots of things he wanted to say, but nothing pressing.

He felt like she was pushing herself too hard. That she was doing so much more than what was required of her and not taking care of herself.

Although this walk was probably designed for that purpose.

Movement coming up the sidewalk caught his eye.

The house he rented was on the very outskirts of Cowboy Crossing, but even if it wasn't, at this time of night, Cowboy Crossing was pretty much dead.

The whole community went to bed when the sun went down, basically.

It had been a little bit weird to get used to, since the stores all closed too, but he liked it, he supposed. Now that he was sober at this time of night.

Her step hesitated, and he assumed she'd probably seen him.

He wished he knew what she thought. They'd joked a little in the kitchen this morning. He wanted more of that.

It's what he remembered from his childhood. She wasn't exactly one of the guys, because she never did anything that they did, but he was comfortable with her and didn't feel like he was gonna scare her or that she couldn't handle anything they were doing. She had a level head on her shoulders and took things in turn, dealing with things in a matter-of-fact way that precluded panic or anger.

"Are you checking up on me? Or do you need something?"

"Neither."

She stopped in front of him. "So you're just out here taking in the night air? Looking at the stars?"

"They're beautiful here, aren't they?"

Athena leaned her head back and looked at the sky.

Deep velvet black, sparkling lights, so much easier to see in an atmosphere unpolluted with artificial lights.

"They are."

"Thank you for doing more than expected." There were a lot of other things he wanted to say, but that seemed like a good one to start out with.

"You're welcome." Her face turned back to his, and her eyes blinked. "I'm kinda surprised you noticed."

He swallowed. He deserved that. "Maybe I'm making a few changes."

"Good luck with that." The words came out kind of light, and he felt like she thought he wasn't going to be able to do it.

"You used to have faith in me."

She tilted her head. "Maybe because you were my brother's friend, and I had faith in him, and I just transferred it to you."

"Your brother and I are still friends."

"I know."

"Don't I get the transfer of faith still?"

"I guess I lost it when you thought alcohol was going to solve your problems." Her words were direct, as was her gaze. He wouldn't have expected anything else to come from Athena. That was the kind of person she was. Direct. Straight to the point.

"Did you tell me there was a different way?"

"I believe I did. I'm pretty sure you wouldn't listen to me."

"You're right. I'm sorry. That was a stupid thing to say. I have no one to blame for my problems but myself."

"That's a start."

"It's a start in the direction I don't intend to deviate from."

If she were thinking that he might be going back to what he had been, that this was just a temporary thing, he wanted to make sure she understood it wasn't.

He felt that was key in getting her to trust him. In getting her to want more with him.

"I suppose time will tell."

"How much time?" he couldn't help but say. Maybe he was biting off more than he could chew. He was trying to figure out how to become a dad.

Maybe it was too much to try to figure out how to become a man that was worthy of a woman like Athena.

He laughed at that, because he was pretty sure that Athena wouldn't say that anyone needed to be worthy of her. That was just the way he thought in his head.

"I don't know. How much time do those things take? How much time do you spend doing something before you realize it's what you're going to keep doing? How much time does it take to form a new habit?" She looked back up at the stars, her voice a little muted. "I've heard that once you're addicted to alcohol, the desire for it never leaves." She looked back down. "I guess that's forever."

"Really? Once a man makes a mistake, he pays for it forever?" Surely not.

"You reap what you sow. You can't change it, can't change the seed you put in the ground when it's time for harvest."

"But you can start sowing something else. You can always start sowing something else."

"I guess. But most crops take months if not years to reap the harvest from. Life is no different."

"Then maybe it takes faith."

"Maybe it does."

"So I guess I'm gonna need to find someone who's got a lot of faith."

"I guess you will."

He didn't know what he was expecting. For her to say *hey, that's me*. Or *I could have faith*. Or even acknowledge that he was trying.

He didn't know. He didn't know what he wanted, what he expected.

It didn't matter anyway. She didn't say anything else but turned away from him and walked up the steps and into his house.

Leaving him standing out in the dark, under the stars, alone.

Chapter Eleven

***

"I'm sorry. I didn't realize the baby was going to wake up with a fever this morning." Reagan's voice held regret and tones of worry.

"Of course you didn't." Athena squeezed her phone, worried for Reagan and her little one.

"I have a doctor's appointment for her and was just getting ready to leave. But I wanted you to know I wasn't going to be able to make it to help today," Reagan said, her voice muffled like she was holding her phone with her shoulder while she held the baby.

Athena forced her voice to come out calm and reassuring. "Of course it's okay. That's what I want you to do—make sure your little one is okay, get her the help that she needs. She's tiny, and it's always scary when your baby is sick."

"That's so true. I know I'm going to be early for the doctor's appointment, but I just can't sit around. She's not having any trouble breathing and doesn't seem to be in distress, but with the fever, it's still scary."

"I know. If I thought there was any chance of there being

anything seriously wrong, I would recommend you go to the ER immediately, and I'm sure the doctor would have said that too."

"You're right. They asked me a bunch of questions and then seemed to decide it would be okay to schedule me a regular appointment."

"I'm glad they were able to get you in."

"Me too. I just feel bad that we made plans and I'm not going to be able to help."

"Don't worry about it. People always show up. That's just the way things work." Athena twirled her hair and thought about all the times she'd either showed up to help people, just when they needed it, or when the same thing had happened to her.

Things always worked out.

"I'm sure you know since you're married to him, but Andrew won't care whether the basement is decorated or not. It's just us ladies that want to have it pretty."

"So true." Reagan laughed a little. "As long as the food is good, and there's plenty of it, he'll be happy."

"Agreed. Now take care of the baby and yourself and don't worry a thing about the party. I've got it all under control."

"Thanks."

"Let me know how things turn out," Athena said.

"I will. Thank you again."

Athena swiped off on her phone and stood staring down at her feet.

She'd left Joyce this morning about ten o'clock and had planned to meet Reagan. Now, she'd still go decorate, but she'd do it herself.

An hour later, she had streamers strung from one side of the church basement to the other, had pinned them all in the middle, and was working on blowing balloons up for a cache in the middle.

She had her phone playing music and was singing a hymn at the top of her lungs, something she didn't normally do, but hey, there was no one around and it was a church after all, so she didn't hear the door open and didn't know Preston was there until she finished blowing up a balloon, pulled it away from her face, and he was right in front of her.

She probably wouldn't have let go of it, but she squealed—something she normally didn't do—and jumped, and he reached out to steady her, and she jerked, losing her grip on the balloon, and it blew out with a slobber, bumping into Preston's face before shooting down, touching her knee, then shooting off to the side and landing underneath the chair.

"This is a surprise," she said, sounding breathless.

"Sorry. I didn't mean to scare you."

"My fault." She stood up, went over, and turned her music down. "I couldn't hear. That was way too loud."

"It's okay. I kinda like seeing you being a little loud and a little irresponsible. It's a different look on you. One I like."

She thought of their conversation yesterday, where she'd basically told him he was too irresponsible and that it would take years before he could change that reputation.

She liked having everything in order. Everything sitting right where it belonged, having a schedule and knowing what was going to happen next. She didn't like surprises.

This surprise birthday party for Andrew had been Reagan's idea, but Andrew had always liked surprises when he was younger. She smiled fondly at the memories.

He'd grown up some from those days, of course, but still had a lot of little kid in him.

"I said can I help you?"

She startled, realizing that Preston had asked her twice.

Did she want his help?

There was a lot to do, and she would appreciate help, but...it was Preston.

She liked being with him, and he'd always been so much fun.

Up until the day of the accident.

"Sure. I wasn't going to get too wild and crazy about it. Reagan's the one who wanted all the decorations, and of course, we want it to be a big surprise. I want to do the best job we can, but right now, she's more concerned about the baby."

"She has a fever, and she took it to the doctor, right?"

"Yeah. How'd you know?"

"Small-town gossip." He gave her that cute little boy grin, the one she hadn't seen for years until he'd flashed it a couple of times in the last week. "I was working with Deacon today, and Blair had told him. And apparently, Blair had heard it from her mother who heard it from Reagan who had asked her mother to ask Blair to make sure her brother had supper in case Reagan wasn't back in time."

"Wow. That's quite a grapevine," Athena said, feeling a little bit like she'd really like to be a part of the big happy community like that. But being a nurse who traveled from job to job the way she was, working with hospice, she moved around a lot.

"Are you going to tell me what to do?" Preston spread out his hands. "I'm at your service."

Athena gave him some instructions, and he started moving chairs around and getting tables set up.

After they'd been working quietly together for a bit, he said, "I'm going to ask you something. Is that okay?"

"Of course. You can ask any question you want to."

That seemed weird. He asked her if he could ask a question.

His hand fiddled on the back of the chair in front of him before he picked it up and moved it.

He set it down in the spot where it belonged before he turned back and said, "I was talking to Deacon today, and he said that he was starting a choir. No long-term thing. He just thought it'd be fun to practice a few weeks and sing a few songs in the spring festival. No years-long commitments or anything."

He moved another chair, and after he had set it down, he went to get another one and didn't say anything more.

"Was there a question in there that I missed or something?"

He chuckled, then looked up at her. "No. I guess I was just trying to figure out how I wanted to say this."

She wished he'd just say it. "Do I look like I'm going to bite you or something? Am I that scary?"

"You have no idea how scary you are."

"Oh, stop. You're like twice as big as I am. How in the world could I be scary to you?"

"Your scariness has nothing to do with size."

"I think I'm offended. You said I had scariness."

"Please don't be offended. Because that's scary too."

"Okay, fine. I'm scary. I kinda feel like you're putting off whatever question you want to ask me. Just ask already."

"I'd rather talk about how scary you are. That's actually kind of fun."

"Apparently, I hadn't been scary enough to get you to quit drinking," she said and then wished she hadn't said anything.

But she supposed there was no point in beating around the bush. He'd been drinking for years, and surely, he didn't want her to pretend he hadn't been.

"If anybody could scare me into quitting, it would have been you." The tease was out of his tone.

"I'm sorry. I shouldn't have brought that up."

"Why not? It's not like I want everyone in my life to pretend that I wasn't an alcoholic for a decade. That is my truth, and I need to face it. Although, hopefully I can also be given a little bit of grace, if I say that I've changed."

She jerked her chin. He was right. That was a direct answer to what they'd been talking about yesterday, and she said, "I'm sorry. You're right. If you say you've changed, then I should believe you unless your actions say something different."

He smiled at that and set the chair down with his hands wrapped around the back of it, leaning on it. "I want to know if you'll go to Deacon's choir practice with me."

Her eyes fluttered, and her head jerked up. She'd been in the middle of tying a big blue bow around the net of balloons, and she looked back down, focusing on getting the ribbon to flow just right before she finished and stepped back, looking at her handiwork.

"Looks nice," Preston said.

"Thank you," she said, rolling his question over in her mind.

Of course, she wanted to go with him. She couldn't stop the fluttering of her heart and the eager lift of her chest.

But it wasn't a good idea. Nothing could come of it. There were too many people she knew who had gone down this road and had nothing but heartache to show for it. She wasn't going to do that herself. It was foolishness.

Not to mention, she was only going to be in Cowboy Crossing as long as Joyce needed her.

If she could reconcile Preston with Liam, she'd consider her work a resounding success.

It had never been her intention to develop a romance with Preston.

Even if that's what she'd always wanted. It had been years now that she'd known that what she wanted and what she got would be two different things.

"Okay, I just want to make something clear to you," Preston started.

"Yeah?" She lifted her head, in the process of cutting another length of ribbon.

"I wasn't asking you to go to Vegas and have a shotgun wedding. I was asking if you want to go to choir practice with me. *Choir practice.* Not a lifetime commitment, just six weeks tops, and maybe singing at the festival. I'm pretty sure if you don't want to stand in the front row for that, Deacon will make sure you get tucked in the back somewhere nobody can see you. No binding vows. No lifetime commitment. Nothing that should take you twenty minutes to think about."

"Maybe I can't sing."

"I just walked in on you. I heard you. You can sing. Sounded good." He grinned that cute grin again, and she had to look away.

Part of her really wanted to say yes, but the bigger part of her was sure that spending time with Preston was a really bad idea. Another part of her was suspicious. Why was he asking her anyway? Did he feel like he had to because of Liam and Joyce?

"You know I'm getting paid for what I'm doing with Joyce, right?"

"What does that have to do with anything?"

"I just wanted to make sure. After you agreed to let Joyce move in, she sold her house, and when she spoke with me about it, she said that if you would take Liam, the money that she made from selling her house would pay for her care. She was worried about it running out." Athena ran her hand along the ribbon, judged the length, then snipped it. "So I told her that I would work for her until the end and whatever I made from my regular job along with her house money would be enough. It didn't matter how much money there was or wasn't. I wanted to do that to put her mind at ease." She carefully folded the ribbon into a large bow. "And I was able to speak with my supervisor at hospice and work everything out."

"That doesn't sound like the way things typically go."

"It's not. But Joyce is a special case, not just because she doesn't have any family, but also because..."

"Because of Liam...and me."

She nodded. She couldn't deny that she felt an immediate attachment to Liam because of his stark resemblance to Preston.

"So I owe you more than I thought."

"No. You owe me less. That's what I was trying to say. You don't have to take me to choir practice or do anything because you feel guilty or feel like you owe me or anything."

"That wasn't what that was about. And you're wrong. Because if you hadn't brought Joyce and Liam into my life, it wouldn't have provided the shock I needed in order to put away the bottle for good."

Was it for good? She had to wonder.

She wanted to trust him. Honestly, she did. But every experience she'd had with alcoholics was that they lied. About everything.

Preston had never been a liar. She wanted to believe him.

Preston started moving chairs again, and he didn't look at her when he said, with obvious disappointment, "Don't worry about it. It's obvious you don't want to go. I know sometimes it's hard to say no. There aren't any hard feelings."

Athena felt terrible. She didn't want to hurt him. That was the absolute last thing she wanted to do. But she didn't want to get hurt herself either.

That was selfish.

She thought, had convinced herself, that she'd been in love with Preston for years.

That's why she'd been so hurt and upset when he'd been wasting his life drunk and hungover, not living up to his potential, and not being the person he could be.

But did she really love him?

If her own feelings getting hurt were more important than not hurting his...that wasn't love.

That was selfishness.

That was putting herself first, which was the opposite of love.

"I want to go with you. To choir practice," she said, staring down at her hands, her voice not sounding like hers at all. Timid and scared.

"I was serious. It's no big deal. You don't have to go. My tender feelings can handle it."

"I was serious too." She lifted her head and pulled air into her lungs, enough to make her voice sound strong and businesslike, the way it usually did. "I want to go. Are you still going to take me, or do I have to go by myself?"

She lifted her chin, and yeah, maybe her look was a little challenging, but that's kind of how she felt. She was gonna take a chance; surely he could give her a few minutes to waver back and forth before she did.

"All right then. The first practice is tomorrow."

"I assume the practices are here?" she asked, indicating the church.

"They are. I'll pick you up. Unless you're at my house."

She nodded.

"Are you still staying with Mrs. Hudson?"

"You mean the grapevine hasn't told you that?"

"It has. But I wasn't going to admit that I knew where you lived. It seemed kind of stalkerish."

"It is."

"Did I scare you?"

"I'm the scary one, remember?"

"I'm trying to up my game. I can't let you best me."

"I think I'm more than willing to let you win the scary person contest. If that's what we're having between us."

"Good. I'm pretty sure I'm supposed to be the one winning. Since I'm the man."

"Oh my goodness. That was sexist."

He grinned. And she had to return it. Since he'd known right away that she was joking. She liked that he could read her mind and enjoyed her sense of humor, which was maybe a little unusual.

"Never thought I'd be dating my best friend's little sister," he said, shaking his head as he pulled the legs out on a table and set it up.

"A date? We're going to choir practice. That's not a date."

"Sure is. We're dating. Never thought I'd see the day."

She put both hands on her hips. "You tricked me. You said choir practice."

"What would you call it? I'm picking you up, we're going somewhere. We're going to have fun, spend some time together, and if I'm lucky, maybe we'll enjoy taking a walk in the moonlight afterward, or maybe we'll get some ice cream."

"I can't believe you tricked me like that."

"You'd rather go bowling?" he asked with a lifted brow, probably knowing what her answer would be.

"Of course not. But choir practice isn't exactly something you would like. I can't believe you're not wanting to take your date mountain climbing or something."

His face didn't even cloud. Her heart skipped along, happy.

"That's next week." He grinned. "And this is not some arbitrary faceless, mindless date person. It's you. There's a difference."

Okay, he definitely warmed her heart with that one. That he wasn't just putting in time, going out with the only available female in town.

That made her feel like she might be a little special.

"So." She held the ribbon between her thumb and first finger and pulled it along, feeling its silky softness, coming to the end, and letting it fall before she spoke again. "Are we dating exclusively?"

He looked up from where he was pulling the legs out on another table. "Definitely." He paused for a minute, looking at the leg without moving it. "Did you have someone else you were seeing?"

His voice sounded a little insecure, and he didn't look at her but busied himself with the table again.

"No... Did you?"

"I have a lot of faults, have done a lot of things that I wish I hadn't."

Somehow, she got the impression that Joyce was lumped in with that. Although, she was almost certain that he would say he didn't regret Liam. Liam had turned out to be the instigation that he needed to get out of the situation that he was in.

"But dating two girls at one time has never been one of them."

"I see. I guess I knew that."

He grinned. "I guess you did."

They worked for another forty-five minutes or so, until the basement was decorated just as beautifully as it would have been if Reagan had helped her.

Tomorrow, she'd go with Preston to choir practice. Their first official date. She could hardly believe it. And she had to admit she was a little scared.

Chapter Twelve

Preston's hands were sweating on the steering wheel as he pulled into Mrs. Hudson's house.

He'd seen Athena this morning before he left to go help Loyal, and he'd seen her again this evening before she left.

But this was a little different.

Plus, there was a small wrinkle in his plans.

He was just stepping out of his truck when his phone rang. He thought about not getting it, but when he looked and saw his dad's number, he swiped and put it to his ear.

"Hello?"

"Preston. Do you have a few minutes?"

"I do. Not more than that, though."

"This won't take long. When I'd spoken to you, a little over a week ago, you'd said about wanting to get back into the business. We just had a little shake-up, with some of our top executives moving on to a new startup company, with my blessing, but that leaves a few openings, and while I know you haven't been here for a while, there is nothing that those people have been doing that you can't do. And you did put your time in years ago. I wanted to offer a position to you if you're interested."

Preston took a few minutes to stare into space.

He hadn't been expecting this. He'd been thinking he'd work for his dad remotely, probably on the ground, installing systems and possibly giving estimates. He'd done office work before, and he figured he'd probably do some of that remotely, but this...

"This would be in the office building down in Houston?"

"Of course. I mean, we've talked about opening up branch offices in other places, but we haven't yet."

"I know."

Yeah, his parents would expect him to move to Texas. Not what he wanted to do. And he couldn't do it now, not if he wanted to court Athena. Maybe if they were a little further along in their relationship... He couldn't say for sure. He just knew going to Texas was completely out of the question, not if he was going to develop something with Athena.

But he couldn't tell his dad no right off. After the last decade and what he'd put his parents through, for him to be offered something this good—like he'd never left the company—was far better than he deserved to be treated.

"Can I have some time to think about it?"

His dad drew in a breath, like he wasn't expecting that. Of course not. His dad had offered him a really fantastic opportunity, one that probably wouldn't open up again anytime soon. He should be jumping all over this.

Especially if he was serious about what he had told his dad, that he wanted to get back into the family business in a big way.

His dad had just opened the door and made it possible. He hadn't had the reaction his dad had been expecting.

"Of course. How long do you think you're going to need? A week?"

"Yeah. I'll definitely let you know within a week."

"Okay, thanks. I'll let you go. Call me if you have any questions."

"I will."

They hung up.

Man, he couldn't even believe after all the years that he'd wasted, letting his parents down and screwing off, that they would even give him a chance like this again. And he would have jumped all over it if it weren't for...

He looked over at Mrs. Hudson's house. Sure, he'd basically grown up with Athena, but he really barely knew her.

Was she worth giving up this once-in-a-lifetime opportunity in his family business? If he said no, his parents, especially his mother, would be extremely upset with him.

Was the chance to have some kind of relationship with Athena worth all of that?

He thought about everything that Athena had given, not just to him but to Joyce, a woman she barely knew. How she'd gone above and beyond anything she needed to do for the Hudsons.

He remembered seeing her standing beside Mrs. Hudson at the funeral, a wall of strength for a woman who had just lost her husband.

She absolutely was the kind of woman that would be worth giving up whatever was necessary in order to have a chance at being with her, but *was* there a chance?

It'd taken her a long time to say yes to tonight.

Maybe he would throw this chance in the company away, everything away, and Athena would end up telling him no.

He didn't want to ruin tonight by thinking about those things, so he tried to put that thought out of his head and focus on being the kind of date that Athena deserved and on enjoying himself as well.

He opened the back door of his truck and grabbed the pot he'd brought, careful of the plant that stuck out of it.

He'd gone out on a limb a little with this too, but Athena wasn't a typical woman.

It'd be silly for him to treat her that way.

Hoping he'd made a good decision, he walked up the steps and knocked on the front door.

It opened right away.

He almost laughed, but he kept his face serious. Was she standing there waiting for him to knock? Sure seemed like it. That thought eased the tightness in his chest a little. The idea that she might be looking forward to seeing him.

"Hey, Preston. Come on in. Oh my goodness, what's that?" Athena said as she opened the door wide and held it while he stepped in.

"I thought about bringing flowers, but I thought maybe you'd prefer to have something with roots."

Please let her like it. Please let her like it.

He held his breath and watched her face. Her head tilted, but there was a smile tripping around her mouth, and her eyes sparkled. After a couple of seconds, her teeth flashed, and those golden eyes flew to his.

"I love it!" she exclaimed. "This was such a smart idea. It will last so much longer than a bouquet of flowers, which I totally was not expecting. I wasn't thinking you'd bring anything. We're going to choir practice, for goodness' sake."

"I wanted to bring something. Isn't that what you're supposed to do on a date?"

"It sure is, son. Your mama taught you right." Mrs. Hudson came down the stairs and put an arm around him, squeezing tight. Her figure was slightly matronly, but her eyes were youthful, and her face wreathed in easy, familiar lines as she smiled. She smelled like cinnamon and sugar, and he felt loved and accepted in her half embrace.

He wished his mother was more like Mrs. Hudson. Here, he felt like he could fail and it would be okay; she'd still love him no matter what he did.

With his own mother, there were certain things that needed to be done, or else. Failure wasn't an option. Embarrassing her was even worse.

She wouldn't have liked out-of-the-box thinking like the plant. She would have said he should have brought a dozen roses, just to play it safe.

But he had never been a play it safe kind of guy.

That was part of the reason, when he'd worked for his dad before, he'd been so successful.

He wasn't afraid to take risks.

"So what type of plant is that?" Mrs. Hudson asked.

"I've seen these at clients' homes. I think it's a ponytail tree?" Athena's eyes went to him, questions in them but excitement as well. If her flushed cheeks and bright eyes were any indication, his gift was a success.

"That's right. I don't know why seeing it made me think of you. This will grow inside or outside, and it says you don't have to water it consistently. I thought it might work with your job."

She tilted her head, a half smile on her face. "You really put some thought into this."

"I did."

He didn't add that he wanted it to be perfect for her. That he wanted to get her something no one else ever had, something perfect she didn't even know she wanted.

He almost got her a puppy. He laughed at the thought.

"What's so funny?" Mrs. Hudson asked.

"It was either this or a puppy."

"Oh my goodness. Tell me you're joking," Athena said, a hand going to her chest.

"Not joking. I was on the verge, and then I decided that if for some reason you didn't want a puppy, I was probably going to get to keep it, and while Liam would probably really love it, I'm still adjusting to being a father. I'm not sure I'm ready to be a pet owner as well."

"You had a cat on your porch."

"That's a stray that comes around. I feed her. That's about it."

"You feed her every day. I've seen you."

"True."

"I'm pretty sure feeding an animal every day, on a consistent basis, means it's your pet."

"It has to have a name in order to be a pet."

"Okay. Fine. Shelley. You can call her Shelley. Now she has a name, and she's officially your pet."

"Shelley? What in the world made you choose that name?"

"Hey, you had all kinds of time to name the cat, and you haven't, so don't even complain about the name I came up with."

"Okay. No complaining. But can you tell me where in the world you pulled it from?"

"Sure. She has orange spots over a white base, and one of the spots looks like a seashell. Hence, Shelley."

He shook his head. "All right. Shelley it is."

"Wow. That was quite a sight to see. You went from a non-pet owner to pet owner in the space of just a few seconds. I hope you can handle it." Mrs. Hudson smiled and shook her head. "Kids nowadays." She patted Athena's arm. "I'll be in the library if you need me. I probably won't be up when you come home. But I'll leave the door unlocked. I never lock it anyway." She stroked the head of the little dog in the carrier that she had on her shoulder.

"Is it okay if I put this on the counter for now?" Athena asked Mrs. Hudson.

"Of course, dear. Put it wherever you'd like. I told you as long as you're here, this is your home too." Mrs. Hudson smiled benignly at Athena, then gave a little wave as she walked away.

"Thank you," Athena said before turning to Preston. "Follow me and we'll take it to the kitchen and give it some water."

Preston followed her down the hall, through the dining room, and into the kitchen, where there was a small light on over the sink. Athena turned on brighter lights when she stepped in and pointed to a side counter.

"You can set it here." She moved to the sink and grabbed a small cup. "I can't believe you brought a plant. I love it." She hadn't quit smiling since she'd seen it, and he believed it. It made his heart feel good and right that he'd chosen wisely.

"Mrs. Hudson seems like a really nice lady to live with."

"She is. I think... I think she's lonely. I'm glad things worked out that I could stay a little longer. Her children include her in almost everything, and she has her grandchildren almost every day after school, but there's definitely a void in her life after losing her husband of so many years. I don't think that's something that you get over quickly."

"I'm sure you're right." He lifted the plant up while Athena put a plastic lid underneath it and then carefully dribbled water around the base of the tree. "Maybe she should sell the farm and move to a retirement community. She might be happier."

"I don't think so. She loves this house, and she loves the farm. I don't know. I think..." Athena looked around and lowered her voice, stepping closer, her chocolate coffee scent familiar and beloved. "I think she might have a romance in the works."

"Mrs. Hudson? She must be in her mid-fifties."

Athena laughed. "That's not old. That's definitely not too old for romance." He could hear the smile in her voice, see it on her face, and he held his hands up.

"I'm sorry. I guess you're right. That just...maybe it's me. It's hard to imagine Mrs. Hudson with anyone but Mr. Hudson. And I guess I just assumed she'd live by herself for the rest of her life, never forgetting Mr. Hudson."

"Oh, I'm sure she'll never forget him, but I think she'd like to share her golden years with someone. There's no rule that says you can only have one great romance in your life."

Athena lifted her brows in question, but he couldn't argue.

"She did everything she could for Mr. Hudson while he was alive, but I think, now that he's gone, he'd want her to be happy and not lonely and sad. I'm sure he would encourage her to find someone else. If he were here."

"I guess."

Preston wasn't too sure about that. He supposed that was probably what love was, wanting the person you love to be happy, even if it meant them finding someone new after you were gone. He didn't want to think about that. He wasn't there yet.

"There. I think that's good," Athena said, stepping back and admiring her plant. "Are you ready to go?"

"I sure am. Um... A slight change from yesterday when we talked about this..."

Athena stopped and turned, a half-smiling, half-apprehensive look on her face. "What's that?"

"Nothing serious. I was telling Joyce that I was going to choir practice, and Liam asked if he could go. Which shocked me, because I didn't know he had any interest in singing, but I said yes, because there is going to be a children's choir that Blair will be working on downstairs. So if it's okay with you, we'll pick him up on our way there. I know that that kind of makes it that this isn't a date anymore if we're taking my kid with us, so can I make it up to you? After the birthday party."

"You don't have to make anything up to me. This is still a date."

"Well, it's not exactly my idea of a date."

"That's fine. It doesn't have to suit your idea or anyone else's. It can just be a different kind of date."

"A date should end with a kiss, and I don't think I'm going to try to kiss my date good night with my kid looking on. I haven't gotten to that point in fatherhood yet."

Athena huffed out a startled laugh. "A good-night kiss? Wow. So I don't have to wonder whether or not that's coming. I've got a warning. Thanks." She held up a finger. "But not tonight."

"That's right. On our real date-date. Whenever that is."

"I'll look forward to it."

He hoped that was true.

Chapter Thirteen

Athena parked in front of the dilapidated house. Before she could wonder whether or not she should get out, the door cracked open, a head poked out and looked both ways, then the figure slid out the door, carefully closing it behind her.

She walked swiftly to the edge of the porch before trotting across the sidewalk and opening the passenger door of Athena's car.

When the head bent down, Athena gasped. "He gave you a black eye!"

She was stating the obvious. Nicole would have been on the receiving end of that blow, and she would have known exactly how hard it was. But Athena couldn't stop the words nor the anger that exploded in her chest.

She fumbled for her phone. "We are calling the police."

Nicole plopped down on the seat beside her and put her hand over Athena's, pushing down. "No. I won't go with you if you call."

"You can't let him get away with this." Tears pricked her eyes as she looked at her friend's face. "I can't just sit here and let him do this to you." Her throat clogged, and she couldn't form words. They would come out in an angry jumble, then she would be the one crying rather than Nicole, who seemed weirdly calm.

Athena had suspected when Nicole called her and asked her to pick her up tonight and told her it was an emergency that this might be the reason.

"It was your husband, correct?" She didn't want to jump to the wrong conclusions, because while Nicole's husband had yelled and thrown things during drunken tirades before, he'd never actually hit Nicole.

"Yes. It was Brandon. But he didn't mean to."

"How can you not mean to punch someone in the face?"

"He was drunk. He didn't know what he was doing."

"You always make excuses for him."

"And you always argue with me. I just want compassion."

Athena closed her eyes. She did have a tendency to want to boss people and tell them how to fix things, instead of just lending a shoulder and patting people on the back.

But she wanted this fixed.

If someone knew a solution that would help her and they didn't tell her, Athena would be upset. She'd rather have a solution than compassion.

She reached over, putting her arm around Nicole.

Nicole leaned toward her, laying her head on Athena's shoulder while Athena wrapped her other arm around her and held her tight.

"I'm sorry. It just makes me mad. Because I love you and I hate seeing you hurt." She closed her mouth. She wasn't helping.

She hated seeing her friend put down, insulted, belittled, and not allowed to do the things she was good at. Not getting credit for the things that she did right, enduring constant criticism, and constantly being told how she wasn't good enough and how she didn't meet Brandon's standards and how everything that went wrong in his life was always her fault.

That was bad enough.

But then he did this to her.

Athena tried to keep her blood from boiling, but it bubbled like lava in her veins.

She forced her words to be calm. "I'm sorry. You're such a beautiful person. And so talented. And someone I've always looked up to."

"Thanks." After a bit, Nicole lifted her head. "If you don't mind, maybe we can go? I don't want to be here if he wakes up." She bit her lip, chewing on it as though the idea of him waking up worried her. "Usually once he passes out, he doesn't, but I know he'll be mad to find out I'm gone. At least until he sobers up."

Athena tried to bite the words back, but they came out of her mouth anyway. "Are you sure you don't want to call the police?"

"No. I know he's going to get better. I know he's going to quit. He says he will. I know he wants to. I don't want him to have a criminal record that will follow him the rest of his life. When he finally gets sober, it will hinder him. I don't want to do that to him."

"Why don't you leave him?" Even while she said that, Athena didn't necessarily believe that was the right decision, either.

"Because I made vows. And I'm going to keep those vows."

Athena pressed her lips together. She couldn't argue with that. This might be one of those times that she found that really hard to agree with, but what did "for better or for worse" mean?

"You know, I always find it so funny that you are one hundred percent okay with me calling the police and reporting him and having him arrested and put in prison and prosecuting him, but when I say I can't leave him, you don't argue with me."

"I guess I see a difference in justice. If you call the police, he will get what he deserves, but you're not breaking any promises. If you stay with him, you're keeping your word, even though a lot of people would say you don't have to. I can admire that."

"You can admire it and also disagree with it, but I know you won't judge. Even though you seem to be physically incapable of not giving me advice, I know you're not going to judge me for the decisions that I make."

Athena gave a thin smile. That was true. She did have a tendency to be bossy and throw out commands or thinly veiled suggestions, but she would never get angry at someone for not listening to her, because they had the right to make their own decisions.

It was her responsibility as a friend to love them anyway, whether or not she agreed with them.

Sometimes, she had to remind herself of that.

"And you also won't give me a hard time for having to come pick me up. Thank you. You're one of the few people who've stuck by me through this."

"Honestly, I have to admire you for continuing to believe in Brandon, because I'd given up hope on him years ago."

That was the truth. Maybe she shouldn't say it because it might be discouraging to Nicole.

"I can't say that I would go back and do the same things over again. If I knew then what I know now, I wouldn't have married him to begin with. But now that I have, I can't quit just because it's not easy."

"I understand." Athena had to say, "Part of me agrees."

There were no children involved. It made her agreement a little easier.

"I'm sorry you're going to be late for your brother's birthday party."

"It's okay. Andrew will understand; in fact, he wouldn't want me to do anything else. I told Mrs. Hudson to let everyone know that I'll be coming but won't be there to start with."

She hadn't told Preston. Honestly, she wasn't quite sure where she and Preston stood with each other.

He'd said there would be a "real" date and he was going to kiss her, and her heart had almost jumped out of her chest.

But the more she thought about it, the more she figured he was probably joking. After all, if he wanted to kiss her, why hadn't he just done it last night? Why talk about it?

Normal people didn't sit around and talk about kissing at some date later in the future, they just did it.

It kind of made her feel like either he didn't want to, but he thought she did so he was doing what she expected without actually having to kiss her, or he had just been joking about it all along. An odd thing to joke about, true, but she supposed it was possible.

She just couldn't think of any other reason.

She spent more time than she was comfortable admitting thinking about that last night.

And when she'd been with Joyce today, she hadn't seen him. Joyce had said he'd already left, going to Loyal's. Probably putting that security system in.

"That's an interesting smile," Nicole said, startling her.

"Sorry."

"Don't apologize. I'm not sure I've ever seen you smile like that before. I think Athena, cool and always in control, has actually fallen in love." Nicole smiled, although there were still shadows in her eyes, and Athena couldn't shut the subject down, because she was happy that Nicole was trying to get her mind off her own problems.

Athena wished she would have chosen a different subject to talk about, but she shrugged. "You know Preston."

"Oh my goodness! You're kidding! Preston? Andrew's best friend along with Shane?" Her voice dropped a little on the last name as everyone's always did. Shane's death was such a tragedy. So unexpected, so heartbreakingly unnecessary. He was a hard one for people to get over.

Athena nodded. "Yeah. That Preston."

"You've been in love with him since, like, second grade."

"It might have been kindergarten, but we don't have to get technical."

Nicole laughed. "You're probably right. I remember you talking about him forever and ever, and he had no idea you existed."

"Thanks." Athena said, with a smile, because it was sarcasm. That had probably been her most common complaint in school when she talked about Preston—that he didn't notice her or know she was alive.

"I don't know how many times you threw yourself over my bed, then moaned into the blankets, 'he doesn't even know I'm alive!'"

"I have to hand it to you. You are actually pretty good at imitating me."

"That's because I heard it a million times if I heard it once."

In junior high.

The older she got, the less she talked about him, because she knew a romance between them was out of the question. They were so different. She, serious and driven, and he, the biggest goof-off anyone had ever met.

"I wasn't that bad," she finally said, because she couldn't help defending herself.

"You weren't. It was just the only thing you ever really got dramatic about. Everything else was pretty much straightforward, black-and-white, if you couldn't do it, you found a way around, through, or over, or you dropped it and went on to something else. Preston was the only thing you had a hang-up on."

"I'd like to say he was worth it."

"Well..." Nicole picked at her purse strap, rubbing it through her fingers without really seeming to know what she was doing. "I guess you've seen what happened with Brandon and me, and you probably know that Preston's a bad idea."

"He quit."

"He did? That's great! I hadn't heard. So he's been sober, what, a couple of years?"

"Two weeks." Athena stared out the windshield, but in her peripheral vision, she could see Nicole wilt.

"I don't want to discourage you, but Brandon is always sober for a week, or a month even. I think the longest he went was four months. But he always goes back. Always. I mean, that doesn't stop me from getting my hopes up. But I don't think I'll ever trust his sobriety enough to have children with him."

"That's smart. That's something else that was a surprise. My patient, in hospice right now, is the mother of his son."

"Preston's son? Preston has a son?"

"I know. I didn't know it either. Neither did he."

"That's probably not surprising."

"No. After Shane, I mostly lost track of him, but his life was pretty much a train wreck."

"Understandably so. When something terrible happens, it's not unusual for people to have trouble dealing with it."

Athena nodded, but she always wondered about that. If something happened to her, would she run away from the Lord? That seemed to be what people did. They blamed God and walked away from him.

It never seemed to occur to anyone, but sometimes, hard things happen in life, things people could learn and grow from. And those hard things were actually good for a person, if they handled them the right way.

Would she remember that when it was her turn to go through something difficult?

"You got quiet."

"I'm sorry. I was just wondering if I have the faith it would take to not walk away from the Lord if some big tragedy occurred in my life."

"You do. You have."

"I've never lost my best friend like that."

"But you have me. You're one of the few who haven't abandoned me. You've been like a rock. That's faith. Faith that you're doing some kind of good in my life. Or faith that things will work out."

"I suppose."

"Athena, you're a hospice worker. You see tragedy with every patient you work with. You've never lost faith."

Athena nodded slowly. She supposed that was true. Mr. Hudson's death had been hard, because he'd been a relatively young man, with young grandchildren, a loving wife, and a successful farm, who was a pillar in the community. And yet, God had taken him. She'd wondered why.

But there were always lessons. Always. It was just a matter of opening her eyes to see them.

It was true, none of her patients ever got better. It always ended in tragedy.

"What time was the birthday party supposed to start?" Nicole asked, almost as though realizing the subject was kind of deep and dark for a night where they were supposed to be celebrating.

"Seven. Maybe we ought to see if we can do something about your eye when we get there."

Nicole grunted and turned her head out the window. "That bad?"

"Everyone's going to know someone punched you. Andrew will know who. But I guess no one else will."

"I can't say I ran into a door or fell down on the back of a chair?"

"If you want to lie, I suppose that's believable."

Nicole swallowed. "No. I haven't lied. And I won't start. What's the point in keeping my vows if I'm going to lie in order to do so?"

"Good point."

"I guess I'd just be careful with Preston. Sobriety for a couple weeks isn't a cure."

The conversation had come full circle, and Athena nodded. She already knew that. She knew she'd be taking a chance even if he'd been sober for years. There was always the chance he'd go back.

She wasn't a very big risk-taker. That seemed like a huge risk to take. A risk for the rest of her life.

Chapter Fourteen

Preston stood at the back of the group of people who were congregated on either side of the door. His eyes swept the faces, looking once more for Athena, although he knew she wasn't there, before Madeline said, "Loyal just texted me. He said that he just picked Andrew up, and so far, so good. Andrew thinks they're going to be stopping here at the church to pick groceries up for Pastor Gus before heading to the feed store for the single dads' meeting."

Preston had chuckled at that. Neither Andrew nor Loyal were single dads, but they still called it the single dads' meeting. In fact, most of the men at the meeting were married.

It should be called the guys' night out or something.

For about the millionth time, he thought about calling Athena, but he wasn't sure exactly where they stood, and he didn't want to overstep or push her away by being too pushy.

He was pretty sure she liked him, and he was pretty sure she enjoyed being with him, but he wasn't entirely sure exactly what that meant. Did it give him the right to call and ask where she was, or would she consider him a stalker?

His eyes brightened when Mrs. Hudson came in the back door across the room and set several packages down before taking off her coat.

He left the group by the door and walked, as casually as he could, across the basement to the door where Mrs. Hudson was hanging her coat.

"Good evening, Mrs. Hudson."

"Good evening, Preston. It sounded like you and Athena had a good time last night. And your plant is doing well today. It's beautiful. What a great idea."

"Thank you." He took a breath, because he wasn't sure what Mrs. Hudson would think about him asking about Athena. Surely if Athena wanted him to know where she was, she would have told him herself.

That made sense, but he was going to ask anyway.

"You look worried, son," Mrs. Hudson said, her kindly eyes twinkling, like maybe she knew the cause of his worry. "I guess you're wondering where Athena is?"

"I have no idea how you could tell that."

Mrs. Hudson chuckled. "I have boys. They're supposed to be unemotional and brave, but in my experience, most of the time they're neither."

"I guess you're probably right."

He really didn't like to think of himself as being super emotional, but Athena had him tied up in knots, and that was his emotions showing.

"Are you going to tell me?"

"I am. If you let me breathe first."

"I think you're teasing me now. Is she okay?"

"I might be teasing you a little, and yes, she's fine."

He breathed out a breath he hadn't even realized he was holding as his chest lightened. How could he not be worried? Of course, she was an old friend, using "friend" very loosely, since he hadn't really talked to her a lot in the last ten years, but he'd known her, and he supposed he'd liked her okay, for years and years, since they were little.

He wasn't even sure when it had become more. For him.

Of course, she would never notice him. Or at least, that's what he thought.

He didn't know what he had done in order to catch her eye, but he didn't want to lose it. Whatever had convinced her that he might be someone worth liking. Or more. He was definitely hoping for more.

"She had to pick up a friend," Mrs. Hudson finally said, sighing. "I guess this friend and her husband were having a bit of an argument. And from what I understand, her husband...drinks too much." Mrs. Hudson looked sad and contemplative. "Athena asked me to tell you where she was."

"Me?" he asked, jumping on that as a sign that maybe he *was* more. "She asked you to tell me specifically?"

"I'm sorry. Everyone here. She asked me to tell everyone here where she was."

"Oh."

"Sorry. I didn't mean to get your hopes up. She just seemed to think it was a big emergency. And I'm a little worried about her friend."

"Did she mention her friend's name?"

"I believe she said her name was Nicole? I think that's what she said."

Preston's heart sank. He'd been around when Athena's friends had been in and out, and he distinctly remembered Nicole.

She'd been married to an alcoholic.

Because of his own problems, it struck him. Not enough to get him to change course. But he'd seen the disdain and dislike Athena had for her friend's husband, and the lack of respect. Andrew had said that more than once, she was worried that Nicole's life was in danger.

"Was she taking her friend to the hospital?" he asked.

Mrs. Hudson's eyes scrunched up. "I don't think so. I'm pretty sure she was just picking her up. I think she might be bringing her here. But I don't know for sure. I'm not sure Athena did."

Preston nodded. "Thank you."

He thought Mrs. Hudson would walk over and join the groups of people, but she walked toward him instead and placed a hand on his arm.

"She is very fond of you."

Her words made his heart race.

"I'm more than fond of her, I'm afraid."

"I think it's because of Nicole, and maybe another friend or two like her, that makes Athena afraid to be more than fond."

"I understand that. I can even respect and agree with that. She'd be taking a chance on me." Even without the alcohol, she'd have been taking a chance on him. He'd always been a daredevil, unafraid, even eager, to take risks.

"She would." Mrs. Hudson narrowed her eyes though, and in a gaze that just seemed to see into his very soul, she looked at him. Then she smiled softly. "I think it would be a chance worth taking. I don't think she would regret it."

"I'd do my best to make sure she didn't."

"I can see that." Mrs. Hudson nodded thoughtfully. "You're a good man. And I believe you'd be good for Athena."

"She deserves a good man."

"Don't sell yourself short. That's what you are." Mrs. Hudson said that with such assurance he almost believed her. She seemed to indicate that she thought he was good enough for Athena.

He hadn't even come to that conclusion. In fact, he would think Athena was settling if she ended up with him.

"It's not an easy thing to go through what you've been through. And it's not an easy thing at all to overcome an addiction. Especially walking completely away from it. She must mean an awful lot to you, if you're willing to do that for her."

He couldn't let Mrs. Hudson think a lie. "It was probably

knowing that I had a son that was the instigation for me to make the change I needed to make."

Mrs. Hudson nodded. "I see. Even more to admire. But," she said, and her serious look melted slightly away as she smiled a little. "I think Athena had something to do with that as well."

He didn't have to think about it for more than two seconds before he nodded. "I'm sure you're right. I maybe didn't give up drinking for her, but I want her to see what I did and be..." He wasn't sure what he wanted from her.

"Proud of you?" Mrs. Hudson supplied. "Or to love you more for it?"

"Both. Maybe more."

"I think that's enough feelings talk for now."

"That's enough feelings talk for the rest of my life."

"Speaking of, where's Liam?"

"He's playing with your grandkids in the activity room."

"I'm glad he's made some friends."

"Yeah. He likes it here."

"Are you staying in Cowboy Crossing?"

He thought about what his dad had offered him and what he'd always thought he was going to do with his life until it got interrupted. He had to give an honest answer. "I don't know."

It wasn't too long after when Chandler Hudson announced, "Turn the lights off. Gather the children. They're three minutes out."

The kids came running from the activity room, and Liam stood with them in a group while Preston stood in the back. In the dark. Wishing Athena was there.

Andrew was duly surprised when he walked in, and everyone yelled "happy birthday" and started singing. Reagan's huge smile said she was super thrilled to have pulled it all off.

They shared a sweet kiss before they walked to the table where there were a few gifts and a large cake.

Preston was happy for his friend but maybe a little on the jealous side as well.

Both of them had struggled after Shane's death, but Andrew hadn't gotten sucked into the bottomless pit of alcohol.

Still, he'd lost his marriage.

Maybe not over that exactly, but he had, and now he had found a good woman in Reagan, and they were beautifully in love.

Unfortunately, split marriages often left hurts, and Preston was pretty sure Andrew missed his boys tonight, since they weren't there.

Wrong decisions always had consequences.

Preston thought about reaping what he sowed and sowing a new crop.

He wanted to sow a new crop, hoped he was doing it now. Hoped every day he woke up and didn't drink but tried to be a father and a friend and a productive worker and, God willing, a husband.

That hope was dashed a little when he saw Athena walk through the door following a cute little blonde with a huge black eye.

Her eye was almost swollen shut and massively discolored.

Preston's heart dropped to his feet and landed with a splat.

That was probably about the worst thing that could happen to Athena right now. She hadn't seemed to object when he said he was going to kiss her. In fact, maybe he was wrong, but she looked happy about it.

He felt like he was taking a chance. Because he hadn't been sure exactly how she would feel.

But now...now that she'd been reminded exactly how terrible life with an alcoholic could be...

He swallowed and looked away.

There were still people waiting to get cake, and he hadn't gotten a piece, wanting to wait for Athena although not wanting to push in if she had planned to sit with someone else.

Still, he walked over as soon as he saw her. Like he just couldn't stay away.

"Hey," he said, his chin jerking a hello at the blonde before his eyes landed on Athena's golden ones.

She stirred all the deep and perfect feelings in his chest, always had.

There was just a rightness he felt when he was with her that he didn't feel with anyone else.

"Hey. Sorry I didn't call. I just asked Mrs. Hudson to relay my message."

"She did." His eyes dropped back to Nicole. "I don't know if you remember me. I'm Preston." He held his hand out.

The blonde took it, shaking it and saying, "I'm Nicole. And I do remember you." She turned to Athena. "If you don't mind, I'm going to walk over to the restroom."

Athena's eyes narrowed slightly, like she wanted to say something, but then she nodded.

After she walked away, Preston said, "She okay?"

"She is."

"Her husband?"

Athena nodded.

"Are you okay?" he asked, not wanting to breach Nicole's privacy.

Athena nodded. "Her husband's an alcoholic." Her eyes went to his, saying so much more than the words that came out of her mouth.

"I know. Mrs. Hudson told me." He wanted to rub his hands together, pick something up, or just do *something*, but he stood still in front of her. He couldn't convince her to keep trying or to take a chance on him if she'd changed her mind.

It was probably the smart decision for her to make anyway.

"He's never hit her before."

"She's leaving him." He assumed so.

Athena shook her head. "She claims to love him anyway. It's frustrating to see, but there's nothing I can do. She wouldn't even let me call the police and report him. She won't prosecute him. She doesn't want him to have a record." She pursed her lips in agitation. "He doesn't deserve her."

Her voice shook with anger and conviction.

Preston couldn't argue with her. She was right.

"With the alcoholism aside, there are so many marriages that I know of where one partner seems to do all the giving and one partner seems to do all the taking. You could say the same about that one partner—they don't deserve the other one. I wonder why that often seems to be the way it is."

Athena, her eyes scanning over the room, although probably not seeing anything, shook her head. "Life just doesn't make sense sometimes. People don't make sense. The things we do don't make sense. I don't understand that, but I've seen it. You're right." She grunted. "Or in my work, I see a couple who are so madly in love with each other, and one of them is dying. And then out on the street, you see couples like Nicole and Brandon, where if one of them died, it would be a blessing. Why? Why is the couple who's madly in love losing one, but the couple who can't stand each other are completely healthy?" She sighed. "Nicole won't leave him, and Brandon will never die. Not that I'm wishing for him to, just that it seems so unfair."

Her words came out in a jumble, and they weren't articulated as well as he knew Athena could, but he understood what she was saying.

"Life isn't fair."

"Exactly."

"If I were God, things would happen differently. People who were in love would live forever, and someone who is being a jerk in their marriage would end up in your care, freeing the partner and giving them the opportunity to find someone who truly appreciates who they are."

Athena nodded and closed her eyes, smiling a little. "Sometimes, it's men who are married to women who don't appreciate them. It's not always the man."

"Seems like it is most of the time."

"No. I don't think so. Maybe men are just more obviously jerks. Women can be nasty, they just do a better job of hiding it."

That sounded right.

"Are you trying to tell me that I should be looking for what you do when you're alone?" he asked, trying to lighten the conversation little.

"Yeah. That's exactly what I'm saying. I'm a terrible person, and you'd be making a huge mistake with me."

"I disagree."

She looked at him as though wanting to say more, then she sighed and looked away again. "I probably ought to go over and say happy birthday to my brother. Was he surprised?"

"He was. Reagan was happy. They kissed. It was pretty romantic, and you missed it."

"Really? Did someone have to tell you it was romantic, or did you figure that out on your own?"

"Will it change things if I tell you I figured it out on my own?"

"Maybe."

"I guess I can't take credit. I figured out it was romantic when I saw Marlowe and Chandler crying. I'm pretty sure Deacon was brushing a few tears away too, but Blair elbowed him and he pulled himself together."

Athena laughed. "Okay. Now I know you're making things up."

"Yeah. Maybe there were a few misty eyes. Maybe mine was one of them. I don't know."

Athena grinned at him, tilting her head to the side. "I'm not sure whether to believe you or not."

"I'm sorry. Men just can't admit to crying. It's kind of hard to admit to thinking kissing is romantic. Plus, I think I'd rather be doing my own kissing than watching someone else's anyway."

"I'd rather watch."

It was his turn to laugh. "I'm pretty sure you're joking about that."

"Are you?" she asked, her eyes glinting, and for the first time in his life, he thought Athena might be flirting. With him.

He liked it.

"Yeah. Because it's inconceivable to me that someone as amazing as you are would rather watch someone else kiss than participate in her own."

"Maybe you're just lacking in imagination."

"Maybe. I'm gonna test my theory. Soon."

Yeah. There was definitely a jump in the pulse at the base of her throat when he said that. He was pretty sure it was an excited jump but wasn't entirely positive.

"Oh? You have someone picked out on whom you're going to test it?"

"Sure do. I warned her twice. I think she's gonna be ready."

"Oh, you're not going to try to take her by surprise?"

"The girl I have my eye on doesn't like surprises."

"I think you're right about that. She doesn't."

"But that doesn't mean that I don't have a few up my sleeve anyway." He winked at her. "Go ahead. Talk to your brother. I want to monopolize your time, but he might not appreciate that."

Athena's eyes slanted over at Andrew, and he followed her gaze. They happened to look just as Andrew was bending over and Reagan lifted her head up. Their gazes as they looked at each other were sweet, and then their heads moved closer and their lips touched.

There was something weirdly romantic about watching someone else while the woman he wanted to kiss was standing right beside him. It definitely made him want to turn his head away from them and do his own kissing.

"I think he's got some good technique there," he said, knowing it wasn't the most romantic thing he could ever say, but how could talking about kissing not be romantic?

"Really? It makes me feel weird to think about my brother's kissing techniques, but I do like to see them happy."

"He deserves it. He's a good man."

Athena turned, and their eyes met. Maybe she was thinking about him kissing her. Maybe. But she said, "You are too."

Then she turned and walked away from him.
It made him a sap, of course, but he watched her go.

Chapter Fifteen

"Liam said it was a nice day out," Joyce said from her hospital bed.

Athena put the soup that she'd been feeding her away and dabbed the napkin around Joyce's mouth. "It is. So warm for March. It definitely feels like spring."

Joyce's head turned, and her face held sadness as she looked out the window. Maybe a little longing as well.

It pulled at Athena's heart.

It was always hard to see people regretting that they couldn't go and do what they used to do. Wishing they could be out with everyone else. Feeling left out. It was one of the harder parts of her job because normally there was nothing she could do.

But maybe today was a little different.

Maybe she could do something.

"How are you feeling?" She didn't want to make a suggestion that was only going to make Joyce feel worse if she wasn't up to it.

"I'm feeling really well." Joyce's eyes actually glowed. "This is the best I've felt in weeks. I almost feel like I'm getting better," she said, and there was no mistaking the hope in her voice.

"How would you feel about taking a walk? Maybe down to the park, and we could feed the ducks? I think Liam would enjoy that."

"He probably would. Where we come from, there weren't any ducks."

"He and Preston were around the back of the house, working on fixing the stone patio. I can see if they might be willing to knock off and take a break." She stood, grabbing the bowl. "It's too bad we've already eaten. I never even thought, but we could have had a picnic at the park."

"Maybe tomorrow," Joyce murmured.

Athena put the dishes in the sink, and then she went out the back door, standing on the steps.

As soon as Preston heard her, his head jerked up, and his face wreathed in a smile. She had to smile back.

They hadn't talked at all today, and they hadn't spoken any more last night at the birthday party.

She'd ended up staying late helping to clean up, and he'd ended up leaving early with Liam to get back to Joyce.

She'd never had this all-I-want-to-do-is-talk-to-him feeling before. She was embarrassed to think how upset she was when he left.

Not upset at him, just disappointed that she wouldn't get to see him anymore.

His leaving took the excitement out of her evening, and she felt like there was no point in her staying, even though she thought it was really good to get Nicole out, and once people had gotten used to the way she looked, Nicole seemed to have a good time.

For now, Nicole was staying with Mrs. Hudson, but she was determined to go back to Brandon, and while Athena understood, she was scared and sad for her friend.

She put that out of her mind. It was a beautiful day, and hopefully, Preston would take a little time to help her do something nice for Joyce.

"A big part of me wants to believe that you're standing there just because you want to see a big muscular man doing a tough job. But

the more intellectual part of me thinks you must want something."
Preston gave her a smile that reminded her of the boy he'd been and
made her heart twirl. "What can I do for you?"

"Is it that easy?"

"Sure is. Tell me what you want, and I'll make it happen."

"Ew. That's sappy," Liam said.

Preston laughed. "What should I have said? 'What you want,
woman?'"

Liam nodded approvingly. "Yeah. Much better."

Athena shook her head. "He's your son."

"I know. But he takes after his mother's side of the family."

"Oh, please. You cannot blame that on someone else."

"Okay. He's the spitting image of me. We're working on that,
aren't we, kid?"

Liam grinned. "Sure are."

Preston straightened and put his hands on his hips. "I'm pretty
sure you want something other than to goof off with me."

"Joyce is feeling really well, and I have a wheelchair in the back
of my car. I was wondering if we might be able to take her for a walk
and go to the park. Maybe feed the ducks?" Her eyes swept over the
patio which was ripped up, with pieces scattered everywhere. "I see
you're in the middle of something. I knew you were. But I thought I'd
ask anyway. I don't think I can do it by myself."

"How'd you like to go to the park with your mom, Liam?" he
asked, turning to his son.

"Are you coming?"

"Sure. I'm never going to turn down an opportunity to feed the
ducks."

"I've never fed ducks."

"Maybe we can stop at the feed store and grab a little corn on our
way through. There's some carp in that pond that are a pretty nice
size and fun to watch. Although they taste disgusting, so we're
absolutely not fishing for carp." He looked at Liam when he said that,
probably just to make sure the kid didn't get any ideas.

Athena had never had carp, so she had no clue what he was talking about, but she could take his word for it. She didn't want to fish, anyway.

"I might have some bread that we can use."

"Sounds good."

In some places Athena had been, people weren't allowed to feed the ducks anymore, since it made essentially wild animals dependent on people, but in Cowboy Crossing, the people had just decided that the ducks would be something that they took care of. So feeding the ducks was not only done, it was encouraged.

"Are we going to finish this?" Liam asked from where he knelt beside three large pavers.

"We will. Not today though. Depends on how long we stay at the park." Preston brushed his jeans off and said to Liam, "Go ahead and get yourself brushed off. I might even have a kite or two in the basement, one of those two-person kites, even. Maybe you and I can work on that a little if we're at the park for any length of time."

"Cool. Two-person kites?"

"They're a little complicated, and I've never been real successful with them, but maybe I just never had the right partner," Preston said, giving Athena a wink before he ruffled Liam's hair.

"I'm really good at kites. I mean, I only ever flew one once, but I was really good at it. I mean, I would have been really good at it if it hadn't gotten caught in a tree."

Preston nodded. "It's funny how those trees just have to sneak up on you and get in the way, isn't it?"

"That's what happened," Liam said, wonder in his eyes.

"Happened to me, too. Kinda crazy the way that works."

Athena shook her head and went back in the house.

It took about half an hour to get everything ready to go and get Joyce in her wheelchair.

There was no way she would have been able to do it by herself, and there was no way that Joyce could have gone without it.

She'd gone from not being able to keep her balance to not being able to move her feet much at all.

The progression downward was always difficult to watch.

Athena tried to keep the focus on what Joyce could do rather than what she couldn't.

Riding in her wheelchair, closing her eyes, and lifting her face to the sun were all on her list of coulds. For now.

They stopped at the feed store to buy corn, and Liam was practically dancing in place as they parked Joyce's wheelchair by a bench. Athena sat beside her while Liam and Preston walked to the pond and threw corn to the ducks and carp.

"You've done such a good job of raising him. He's such a sweet little boy," Athena said.

Serious. She'd worked with a lot of children who were difficult, and while Liam had been belligerent when he had first come, it hadn't been anything like some of the kids she'd seen. And not to make excuses for his bad behavior, but it was perfectly understandable that the kid was upset because his mother was dying.

It would be hard for anyone, let alone a child.

"I know I messed up. I let him think for years that the guy who was living with us was his real dad." Joyce ran her finger over the edge of her wheelchair. "I shouldn't have. I should have been honest with him from the beginning. Because when that guy left, not only did Liam lose what he thought was a father, he found out that he wasn't really his father at all. It was a double shock. I didn't help, because I was hurt and upset. I didn't make it any easier than what I had to. I wanted Liam to hate him like I did. Looking back, it was stupid."

She lapsed into silence, and while Athena was listening, she also was thinking that Joyce's voice and her overall strength was better than it had been in a long time. Like Joyce had said, this was the best she'd been in weeks.

Athena had heard stories of miraculous recoveries, but she'd never witnessed any herself.

All of the patients that she'd ever gone in to help as a hospice worker had passed away, usually faster than the time that they'd been given.

She could hope, for Liam's sake, that Joyce was the first to have a miraculous recovery.

That might put Preston in an awkward spot.

He didn't seem to have feelings for his ex, but they shared a child together; there had to be something there.

She swallowed and forced her shoulders to relax. There was no way that she would hope anything ill on anyone, just to make her own life easier.

Plus, after being with Nicole yesterday, seeing her eye, she knew Preston was anything but a sure bet.

"I think everybody makes mistakes, especially when we're young. We look back on our life and wish we could do things over."

"That's for sure. That's just one of many regrets for me."

"I have things like that too."

"Oh yeah? When I look at you, I see someone who has everything together."

"I guess I go through a lot of effort to look like that. But nothing's ever what it seems, is it?"

"What do you regret?"

Athena played with the kite bag in her hand, folding it into a tight little square. "I regret the times I wasn't a better friend. I regret the times I was selfish and only thought of myself and I hurt people because I was determined to get my way. The times where I had an opportunity to do something new, and I was too scared to reach out and take it." A memory flashed across her brain, so bright and vivid it was like it was yesterday. "Andrew backpacked across Europe, and he offered to take me with him. But doing that seemed silly and foolish to me, and I told him no."

She'd often wondered if she and Preston might have gotten together if she had taken Andrew up on his offer. Maybe they would have decided they couldn't stand each other, and she wouldn't be looking at him now, admiring his easy conversation with Liam, the way he treated the kid like an adult but not in a brusque way, the way he was firm with him, completely establishing that he was the authority, but not in an authoritarian way. He was so good with him. No woman could watch him and not admire that and think he'd make such a great father and a good husband.

"Did Preston go with them?"

She'd forgotten that Joyce knew Preston and Andrew were good friends.

"Yeah. And Shane."

"Yes, Shane. That's a regret."

"I'm sure. I know Andrew wishes they'd used ropes. But they wanted the challenge."

"And they thought they were invincible."

"That's true."

"That's something this tumor has taught me. I always thought of my life as something that was unending. I always thought that way. That death was far off, and I had plenty of time. If I would have known how little time I had, I would have done things a lot differently. You just don't know. And even if you do know, it goes by faster than what you think."

Her hand, resting on the wheelchair arm, lifted to her face and smoothed hair back from her cheek. Troubled.

"All the things I thought were important, as I look back, aren't. All the people I took advantage of, boyfriends I lived with...I thought they weren't treating me right, but as I look back, I realize I was pretty focused on what I wasn't getting and not nearly as focused on what I could have been giving." She paused and turned her head. "You know what I mean?"

Athena looked down at her lap before she lifted her eyes to meet Joyce's gaze. Joyce had been saying some hard things. Things that maybe she didn't want to hear. "In my work, I see a lot of people at the end of their life. And I think pretty much everyone says similar things. They could have been better. And they don't understand why they weren't. Why aren't we?"

Joyce nodded slowly, shallowly, almost as though she were processing that. Trying to find an answer. But there really wasn't one. It was something everyone did.

"Maybe we just look back and see things differently, forget how hard life is. Maybe we need to cut ourselves more slack?" Athena said.

"I don't like that idea. I want to think I'm better. I want to think I could have done the hard things. That even though someone was unkind to me, I could have shown kindness in return. I just did the easier thing because...it's easier. Looking back now, maybe especially with Liam, but with anyone who has memories of me, I want them to remember me as someone who thought beyond myself. And I'm afraid they won't." She brushed at her lap, even though there was no dirt on it. "I guess we kinda get in a rut, and we just do what we always do. In some cases, because we don't know anything else, and in some cases, because we're scared."

Athena nodded, looking back over the pond where the ducks crowded around Liam and Preston. Liam had moved closer to his dad, wasn't exactly pressing into him, but was much closer than he had been, as though eyeing the ducks with a bit of fear.

Athena could tell him that there was nothing to be afraid of, but he probably wouldn't believe her.

He didn't know that for sure himself, and he almost needed to learn it before he would be unafraid.

Some people never got over their fear, even though it was unjustified.

"But sometimes, fear is a good thing. It keeps us from making mistakes that are stupid and that would hurt us. Without fear, we'd rush into things and regret them. In a multitude of ways."

Fear was what kept her from going all in with Preston.

Would he go back to being an alcoholic?

The first time things didn't work out in his life, or the tenth time

—because there were going to be a lot of hard times and trials in his life from now until whenever he died if he lived any length of time— would he have a setback? Would he turn to alcohol? Would she be making a wrong decision?

"That's true. There's no magic trick to know when our fears are justified and when they're not."

"I guess you're right. Although, we can ask ourselves if it's worth it. You know. The consequences. Are they really as bad as what we think they are?"

"That's exactly what I was thinking. That I avoided doing things, because I was afraid, the things I didn't do because I was selfish. And really, what's a mistake? We say we failed, for example, a 'failed' marriage, but it's not necessarily a failure as much as we can look at it as a learning experience. We figured out what not to do. And now we know. Right?"

"I guess. But when there's children involved, think of Liam and the consequences of you splitting up with who he thought his father was. It hurt and was painful. Something he probably will never get over."

"That's true, but so many kids who are from divorced parents have determined in their hearts they won't do that themselves. Maybe he'll work harder at his marriage because of seeing me fail and knowing how that feels. I'm not saying I want to see him go through painful things. I don't. I don't want to see him go through the death of his mother. But those hard things will make him a better person. If he allows it to."

Athena knew she was right. In a lot of ways. To not do something because one was afraid of failing was not looking at failure in the right way. One should be looking at it as a learning experience. Still, the human condition was such that they tried to avoid pain and too much work.

Two things that needed to be faced head-on if one was to get to the end of one's life and not have regrets.

Maybe it was the warm sun, or maybe she'd just done too much, but Joyce fell silent. It wasn't too much later when Athena looked over and saw that she was sleeping.

She took the small pillow that had been sitting on her lap and tucked it under her head so her neck wasn't bent quite so far, and then she lifted her own face to the sun and thought about her life, and the things that she wanted to do, and the idea of getting to the end of it and stepping into heaven with confidence that God would look at her and say, "Well done."

Chapter Sixteen

Sunday morning, Preston padded down the steps early, intent on getting the coffeepot going and not much else.

He'd wanted to talk to Athena yesterday. To set the time for their "real" date. More than just going to choir practice, but he hadn't gotten the opportunity. Once they'd gotten home, she'd received a text from Nicole, and after making sure that he was okay, she hurried out.

He hadn't responded to his dad, and he was running out of time, but he wanted to at least talk to Athena before he made a decision. Not necessarily to check with her, but he wanted to find out if he could stay. Because he would. He'd walk away from his dad's business, and all the wealth and privilege and prestige that meant, even though he felt like he owed his parents for the last ten years when he hadn't done anything and they'd supported him anyway. He wanted to make it up to them, but his future could be with Athena, and that was more valuable than any company or any position.

He hadn't known what to say, so he hadn't called his dad, and he was supposed to make a decision by this evening.

Today. Today, he would see if Athena would go out with him, and maybe they'd have some privacy to talk.

He tiptoed through the living room, although normally, no matter how quiet he was, Joyce's eyes would open when he was about halfway through.

They never said anything to each other this early in the morning but just exchanged glances.

However, something seemed a little off, and it wasn't only that Joyce's eyes weren't open.

Dawn was just breaking, and the light was all gray blue with barely any color, but...his body felt chilled, and his heart froze.

The figure on the hospital bed was too still. Way too still.

Too quiet.

Too...corpse like.

Preston took a step to the side and reached his hand out, but he already knew what he was going to feel.

Cold. Stiff. No life.

He hadn't expected this seizing of the back of his throat, and the ache in his chest, and the ways his fingers wanted to jerk back until they were behind him and far, far away from the body on the bed. He'd seen this before.

Shane.

Of course, he'd had plenty of time to think as Andrew and he climbed back down the wall, oh so carefully. Oh so aware that it could have been either one of them. Oh so scared it would be.

Of course, the body at the bottom had still been warm.

But it had been just as dead.

He took a breath in and let it out slowly.

He hadn't had very long, not nearly long enough, to get used to all the changes that had happened. Were going to happen now. No time to adjust.

No time to say goodbye.

No time to apologize for what never should have been.

Everything he should have done suddenly balled up in his chest and seemed to expand.

Why hadn't he thought of apologizing?

Why hadn't he thought of telling her not to worry about her child? That he was going to take him, that he'd raise Liam as his son.

He hadn't said that.

The front door opened, and his head shot up. Across the gray light of the room, infinitesimally lighter than it had been ninety seconds ago before his world had shifted, he looked into Athena's eyes.

She must have read the expression on his face, despite the dim lighting, because she said, "I just had a feeling. I couldn't sleep, and I just had a feeling."

He nodded. "She had a good day yesterday. Her last."

"That happens. I realized last night, it happens. Maybe that's what woke me. But before the end, sometimes there's one last good day, and that was it."

She walked over slowly and looked at the body, and then her eyes moved up to him.

"Are you okay?" she asked, and there was so much compassion in her tone he felt his eyes prick.

He wasn't going to cry. He never cried.

Not since Shane.

One of her arms slipped around his waist, and she pressed against him, squeezing him without feeling stifling.

He wrapped both arms around her and buried his face in her hair. He really thought he might cry.

"This feels like too much too soon. I'm not ready."

"Life and death are in the hand of the Lord. He must have decided you were ready. Because the time is now."

He knew she was right. And he knew better than to argue with the Almighty, but it didn't change the fact that he was pretty sure, in this instance at least, God had to be wrong. He wasn't ready. He wouldn't ever be ready.

Chapter Seventeen

The funeral hadn't been as hard as he had been anticipating. Just like several months ago when he'd watched Mr. Hudson's funeral, seen as Athena stood, a wall of support, beside Mrs. Hudson, she'd done the same for him.

Liam had stood between them, and Athena seemed to know when he needed a gentle hand and when he needed space.

She seemed to know the same for Preston—when she needed to run interference with someone who was pushing too hard with questions, and when she could stand back and let him handle it.

All in all, it'd been a hard day, but the funeral was over, Joyce had been laid to rest, and the last three nightmarish, sleepwalker days were over.

Athena was in the kitchen now, and Liam sat in front of the TV.

Before Preston had come out and sat down on the porch step, he'd asked Liam if he wanted him to sit down beside him, and Liam shrugged his shoulders and shook his head, and Preston had given him a hard look before leaving him alone.

Kinda crazy how sharp a turn his life had taken in the last month.

He felt like it was probably a good direction for the most part, but it made him sad that Joyce had had to die in order for him to see what was right in front of him.

With Joyce's appearance and the knowledge that he was a father, and the picture of his life, so much shorter than he had thought when he'd started it, then Joyce's death and coming to grips with Shane's, he knew he needed to start making some smart decisions.

He leaned his arms on his knees and lined up his fingertips, pressing them together. He didn't turn when he heard the door open, then close softly.

Maybe he imagined it, because it was faint on the breeze, but he thought he smelled a light dusting of chocolate mixed with coffee. It went down good in his soul. A balm over the chaos and pain, pain that he might have numbed with alcohol, but he hadn't even considered it, although the thread of longing was there.

He didn't hear footsteps and he didn't turn to look, but he could picture her in his mind, her hands behind her, her back leaning against the doorpost, looking out in the darkness with him.

He didn't need to see her, he didn't even need to touch her, although he wanted to. It was enough that she was there.

He didn't know how long they were like that, him sitting, her standing behind him, but it felt like hours went by, yet only a few minutes in some ways, too.

A song had been running through his head. One they'd sung just for fun in choir practice. The words sifted through his thoughts, and it just seemed perfectly right and natural to lift his voice in the night air.

> *Nearer, still nearer, close to Thy heart,*
> *Draw me, my Savior—so precious Thou art!*
> *Fold me, oh, fold me close to Thy breast;*
> *Shelter me safe in that "haven of rest";*
> *Shelter me safe in that "haven of rest."*
> *Nearer, still nearer, nothing I bring,*
> *Naught as an offering to Jesus, my King;*

When his voice trembled on the second verse, hers joined him, soft but confident, bolstering him with her spirit.

It was funny how close a person could feel to someone his voice was blending with. No more comforting feeling than to have their voices mingle and become one.

Two voices. One sound.

Soothing and sweetly beautiful.

Athena came over and put her hand on his shoulder.

Chapter Eighteen

The next day, hospice came, and by dinnertime, all evidence of Joyce's presence had been removed from his home.

He didn't see Athena, but it was probably better that way. He spent the day with Liam, whom he'd allowed to stay home from school.

They alternated between playing video games, watching movies, and spending the bulk of their time on their knees with their hands in the dirt in the backyard, working on the patio.

He wasn't sure how Liam felt about it, but he liked the activity better than he liked the mindless numbness.

Someone had said time healed everything, and he supposed it did.

It wasn't that he needed healing from Joyce's death as much as her death had completely changed his life and his thinking, and maybe the way a bone that has to be broken in order to be set properly, he just felt sore and a little fragile.

Not that he would ever admit it.

He hadn't forgotten the deadline for his dad, although when he'd called, he'd gotten his voicemail.

He hadn't even told his parents they were grandparents, and he wasn't feeling up to doing that, either.

It was a relief to get the voicemail.

He left a message saying that there had been a death and a funeral, and if possible, he'd like a little more time to make his decision.

Maybe it made him a coward, but when his dad called back, he didn't answer the phone.

"Are we going to choir practice tonight?" Liam asked, looking up, dirt on his cheek from where he'd rubbed his face, his eyes red, his clothes filthy.

"You want to?" He hadn't even considered it. He'd figured right now his main responsibility was getting Liam through whatever he needed to get through. He had no idea what that even was.

He supposed it could involve counseling and other things that might help, although right now, he felt like them just spending time together was probably the best thing.

"Yeah. I want to get out of the house."

"We can. We don't have to go to choir practice, though, if you don't want to."

"I do."

Preston nodded. "Okay. We'll go. I guess we better quit here, go inside, and grab a bite, so we don't have to sing loud to cover the grumblings of our stomachs."

Liam smiled, but he didn't quite laugh.

It probably shouldn't have surprised Preston that the kid wanted to go to choir practice. He'd asked to go when he found out about it, and he did enjoy singing.

He supposed it helped that Liam's friends were there too, but maybe there was just something about singing that helped heal soul-deep hurts.

That was probably why God commanded them to do it. He found, when he bothered to think about it, that God's commands often had a basis in what was best for a person.

But maybe like eating Brussels sprouts, what was best for person wasn't always what a person wanted to do.

Athena would be at choir practice.

The thought made his heart beat faster. He almost looked over and told Liam thank you.

He figured it wouldn't hurt to laugh, but it might be just a little bit too soon for a joke like that.

Regardless, the night had suddenly gotten brighter.

———

ATHENA WALKED into the choir practice beside Mrs. Hudson, her heart heavy.

She always felt a little down after losing a patient.

But Joyce was slightly different. Not only had she lost what had felt like a friend, but there was no need for her to go to Preston's house anymore.

She missed him.

She wondered how Liam was doing.

To make her feel worse, Nicole had gone back to Brandon, and Athena had bit her tongue and watched her leave.

She'd have a new assignment soon.

Typically, the agency gave her at least a week between patients.

In this job, it was easy to burn out.

Had she reached that point?

Normally, it was natural to feel down when she lost a patient. But this felt different.

Maybe because of all the other things going on, or maybe because she was just ready to move on.

Or maybe it was something else entirely.

Normally, she didn't wallow around, but she couldn't seem to help it.

She and Mrs. Hudson both sang alto, so they went to their section and chatted with the ladies in their group.

It hadn't taken long, about two seconds, after Athena walked in for her to know that Preston wasn't there.

She hadn't really expected him.

His focus was almost certainly on Liam right now. That's where it should be.

She'd no sooner thought that than the door opened, and Liam and Preston came in, walking up the aisle.

His eyes searched the choir area until they landed on hers.

Caught staring, she smiled at him. A little smile. Cognizant that he probably had a hard day. Definitely she was surprised to see Liam and him out.

He smiled back, his own grin muted, and she looked at Liam, her brows raised, before she looked back at him. Asking without words if Liam was okay.

He gave a small nod and made a little gesture with his hands that made her think that he was saying they were here because of Liam.

She smiled and nodded.

Deacon stood up in front of the choir, looked at his watch, and said, "We're waiting just a little bit longer, because Pastor Gus isn't here. I was expecting him, and I hate to start without him."

"A couple of times, he held his sermon up because I wasn't there, so I guess we owe him this," Clark said with a bit of a smirk.

Marlowe, sitting with the sopranos, looked over at her husband. "Gable, he never waited his sermon on you."

"He sure did. After he gave the sermon upstairs, he'd tell my parents he'd wait on me downstairs, and I'd get a second one. Couple of times."

Everyone laughed. Clark had been quite a character when he was younger.

He was still quite a character.

Liam turned and went downstairs where Blair was working with the children's choir, and Preston walked to the men's section.

The last conversation that she'd had with Joyce weighed heavily on Athena's mind. She wasn't sure exactly what decisions she'd made from it, if any, but she knew in her life she'd made a lot of decisions based on fear and selfishness rather than on what the Lord might have her do, and she hoped she was brave enough to step out and not let fear and the temptation to put herself first continue to dictate what she did.

Like Joyce had pointed out, she didn't want to get to the end of her life and regret it.

With that thought, she determined that she would wait for Preston after choir practice and see if he truly wanted to go on a real date.

Her stomach cramped at the idea of asking, but that was fear, and while she wasn't entirely sure that Preston was the man for her, she knew she liked him and wanted to spend time with him.

Hopefully, that was enough for now.

Unfortunately, Pastor Gus never showed up for choir practice, and at the end of practice, Deacon said, "I'd appreciate it if anyone that could would meet with me for a few minutes before you go home. I think it might be time for us to go visit Pastor Gus."

Athena hadn't been around much, but she knew that Pastor Gus had lost his wife last year, and while it was perfectly natural for him to grieve, the grieving had seemed to go on way too long. Some people said the children were suffering and the church should do something about it.

No one wanted to see him lose his children, so no one had reported him to any government agencies, while the church ladies were trying to do what they could, since they felt that even a bad parent was better for a child than losing both of their parents.

Athena's heart sank though, because she couldn't stay. She didn't know where her next assignment would be, and she might not be around to help. She didn't want to volunteer for anything she couldn't follow through on.

But that meant she was going to have to wait for Preston, because she was pretty sure he'd be staying to see if he could lend a hand.

That meant if she wanted to talk to him, it would be obvious, since she'd have to wait for him. She couldn't just kind of run into him and make it look like an accident as they walked out of church.

Fear-based thinking again.

Determined to be brave, she lingered as long as she could, chatting with anyone else who was moseying out, until finally she was alone. She walked out the church door and stood on the steps.

It was obvious she was waiting.

She supposed that was okay.

Preston would know that she wanted to be with him.

It felt like forever until the men started coming out.

Thankfully, Preston was the second man out.

He was hurrying so fast he almost went right by her, his eyes lifted and scanning the parking lot. Which was odd since he'd be walking home.

Liam was by his side, and it looked like the boy was smiling. If not laughing with a little boy—she thought it was Clark's son—who walked beside him.

Preston glanced at her and looked away before he yanked his head back. "Athena. I...was looking... What are you doing here? Why aren't you on your way home?"

"I wanted to talk to you."

There were still men coming out the door, so Preston said, "Let's walk down the stairs and away from the church a bit."

"Okay. It won't take long."

"Well, I kinda wanted to talk to you, too."

They walked in silence to the edge of the parking lot, Liam saying goodbye to his friend and walking along, too.

When they stopped, Liam said, "Can I keep going? It's not that far to the house."

Preston pulled the key out of his pocket. "No stove or fire until I get home, okay?"

Liam's eyes brightened, and he held his hand out, taking the key. "Okay."

"And don't lose that."

"I won't. I'll put it on the counter when I get in."

"Okay."

His house was only a block or two down from the church, and he could see it from where they were standing, so Athena knew it wasn't too big of a deal, but Liam's eyes were excited and there was a spring in his step as he walked away.

"Looks like he's doing pretty well," she said after he was out of hearing distance.

"Yeah. I was a little worried about him, still am, but I thought he would take it a lot harder. Maybe he just had time to get used to it. I don't know. Or maybe he's a kid and kids are resilient. Or maybe he's internalizing it all and he'll end up being a serial killer."

"Let's hope not," Athena said, not joking.

"I know. Terrible thing to joke about, but I figure when he's ready to talk about it, he will. And I think he might even want to go to school tomorrow. He's the reason we're here tonight."

"I thought that's what you were hinting at when you walked in."

"Yeah. I was really happy he wanted to go, but I wasn't going to suggest it myself." He paused and looked down, shoving his hands in his pockets. "I wanted to see you. I've missed you."

Yeah, that made her heart tremble with a good kind of happiness. And it made it easy for her to admit the truth as well. "I've missed you too. In fact, that's why I waited outside to talk to you tonight."

"To tell me that you miss me?"

"No, smarty-pants. To see if you wanted to do something with me. Like...the date we talked about."

"Yes." He didn't hesitate.

Which made her smile. It also made her feel like he definitely wanted to and wasn't just giving her a yes because he didn't know how to tell her no. Which would be worse than an actual no.

"I don't know how long it will be until I get my next assignment. And I don't know where it will be."

"Then tomorrow. Let's do it tomorrow."

"Liam?"

Preston pressed his lips together. "Maybe I can see if he can go over to Clark and Marlowe's after school, whether he goes or not, and play there. I think he would enjoy that."

"That's fine. Why don't you see first, before you make solid plans. Liam needs to come first right now."

"I agree. But that's part of why I wanted to talk to you."

"Oh?" She didn't see how she had anything to do with Liam. Other than a small connection to his mother.

"Tomorrow. We can talk about it tomorrow. Even if Liam doesn't want to go to Clark and Marlowe's, maybe you could come to my house. I'll cook."

"You cook?" she asked, raising her brows. She hadn't seen him make anything but sandwiches the entire time she'd been there. Of course, to be fair, every time she was there, she cooked something, so he hadn't had to.

"Sure do. I can make hot dogs and baked beans. And if you want to get really fancy, I can add macaroni and cheese to the menu as well. I also make really good store-bought pudding. And I know how to add chocolate sauce to it, which makes it even better."

"That sounds like a lot of sugar. Pudding and chocolate sauce."

"It's no different than ice cream and chocolate sauce."

She scrunched up her nose. "Okay. I think you're right about that. It just isn't cold, and somehow, that makes a difference."

"Got it. I'll freeze your pudding."

"Wow. You really aim to please."

"Athena. I don't think you have any idea."

She stared at him, her mouth open. He was serious. And she didn't know what to say.

A car went by, and she looked away.

She wanted to be more with Preston. But she was also scared. Probably all of those years she convinced herself he was a bad bet. Or maybe it was just the idea of changing.

"So, how about I just show up at your house at seven. And if we go somewhere, that's fine, and if we don't, I'll be there."

"That hardly seems like a date if I'm not picking you up."

"It's a modern-day date. You know, where women drive themselves and stuff."

"I don't think that's the kind of date you want."

She grinned with him. "I guess not. But it's the kind of date we're going to have, and I'm going to be happy with it."

"Thanks." He looked down. "I appreciate you letting me put Liam first... I...I also appreciate you not seeming to hold it against me that I have a son."

"It was a surprise. And I suppose it did take me a couple of days to think about it. But water under the bridge."

"True. I had no choice but to take responsibility, although it didn't matter whether I had a choice or not. I wanted to."

"I admire that."

"Thanks." He looked around and spotted her car parked not too far away. "Come on. I'll walk you to your car."

Athena smiled, and they started off together.

"Would you mind texting me when you get home?"

"Why?"

He shook his head. "No reason, I guess. Just to let me know you got there safely."

"Oh. Sure." She liked that. That he was concerned about her. She read it like that meant he cared. Which made her happy. In a warm and sweet kind of way.

Whatever happened tomorrow, she had a feeling that it was going to define the rest of her life.

A lot of pressure to put on a date, but she couldn't shake it.

Chapter Nineteen

The next day at four o'clock, Athena was helping Mrs. Hudson clean out her kitchen pantry when her phone buzzed with a text.

She glanced at her phone, after pulling it out of her pocket, using a hand to steady herself as she stood at the top of the stepladder she'd been using to wipe off the top shelves.

There's been a little change of plans. Liam is at Clark and Marlowe's, but the men have gone to Pastor Gus's to take him for an intervention.

Athena was wondering what in the world that had to do with anything when a second text came.

Athena grunted a laugh, and Mrs. Hudson looked up from where she had finished wiping the bottom shelf and was putting her Tupperware containers away.

"What's so funny?" Mrs. Hudson asked.

"They're staging an intervention with Pastor Gus, which is not what's funny."

Mrs. Hudson stopped with a blue lid in her hand. "It's about time. Something needed to be done. He's had plenty of time to grieve, plenty of time to heal, and those children need their father." She nodded her head decisively as she set the blue lid on the stack with the rest of the blue lids.

"The funny thing is Preston has volunteered him and me to watch the children while the men do the intervention."

"Oh boy, that is funny. Those kids can be quite a handful. Pastor Gus has been letting them run wild. I think he feels bad that they've lost their mother and isn't disciplining them." Her brows came down in a worried line. "Do you think you can handle it?"

"I'm not sure. I guess we'll die trying."

Mrs. Hudson chuckled. "I think what you're saying is you'll do anything to be with Preston."

"Mrs. Hudson, you are exactly right."

They laughed together.

She sent a quick text back to Preston.

"I hate to leave you high and dry, Mrs. Hudson," Athena said. "But he's going to be here in ten minutes."

"You'd better go get yourself fixed up and presentable," Mrs. Hudson said with a little chuckle. "I'll be fine here."

"I'll leave, but I want you to wait and let me put the stuff on the top shelf."

"It's a deal. I won't go on the stepladder. That's the whole point of doing it with you anyway."

"Thanks." Athena climbed down off the stepladder, and Mrs. Hudson straightened. She stepped toward Athena and put her arms around her, wrapping her in a big cinnamon-scented hug. "I really enjoyed having you here with me. I've even found myself praying that your next assignment will be in Cowboy Crossing or somewhere close, and you'll stay with me."

"Mrs. Hudson, I think we both know that if I leave, someone else might be persuaded to come. Not move in, but maybe spend a little more time here."

Mrs. Hudson's cheeks pinkened, and her blue eyes looked a little guilty. "That's supposed to be a secret."

"I don't think your children know. I think they're expecting that you're going to have a romance with the big-time farmer down the road. But I know that's not where your heart is."

"My heart's on the farm. Always will be. But you're right. That big rancher dude doesn't hold a candle to the fellow I found." She sighed. "I'm worried everyone will think it's too soon. I'm also worried that he's not the kind of man anyone expects me to be with. Do you think the children will be okay with that? They're not used to being around a man who doesn't work with his hands."

Athena had never seen Mrs. Hudson uncertain before. Normally, she had a smile and words of wisdom for just about everyone.

Mrs. Hudson stooped down and put a hand on her little dog who was sleeping next to the flour canister on the floor.

"I think you've raised your children well. I think, more than anything, they want you to be happy. When they see how happy that man makes you, they'll do whatever it takes to get to know him and accept him as one of them. Even if he is different." Athena believed that with all her heart. Mrs. Hudson had good boys.

Her lips turned up, and her face wrinkled in well-worn lines. "That's what I've been telling myself. But I worry. I know that farmer is the kind of man they would expect me to be with, years from now, when it's appropriate for me to look for someone else. I don't want to disappoint them."

"They won't be disappointed, Mrs. Hudson. They'll be happy for you."

"I'm sure you're probably right. The things we worry about that never come true, right?"

Man, could Athena relate. She'd been thinking of fear so much lately.

"We waste so much of our lives worrying about stuff that just never happens. You'd think I'd have learned that by now at my age, but I guess there's a lot of things we need refresher courses in." Mrs. Hudson shook her head at her own foolishness. Then she brightened. "Go on, child. Go get yourself ready to go. Preston's a good man. You'll do well by him, and he'll do well by you."

Athena gave Mrs. Hudson another quick hug, patted her dog on the head, and skipped out of the room. It had been a long time since she'd skipped anywhere, but her heart was light, even with the sadness that had taken place and even with the things that were going down with Pastor Gus.

How could she not be happy? She was going to spend the evening with Preston.

Even if it was with six kids.

———

Preston figured maybe if he'd had any idea of what the evening was actually going to entail, he probably wouldn't be nearly as excited about it as what he was when he pulled up to Mrs. Hudson's driveway and got out of his pickup.

He had no idea how difficult it would be to watch six children, but it pretty much proved that he'd do anything in order to spend time with Athena.

He hoped she'd figure that out.

Maybe it said the same thing about her.

He had his hand raised to knock on the door but hadn't begun when it opened, and Athena stood there, smiling.

"Hey there," she said. He'd never seen such a goofy grin on her face.

"Hey yourself." He figured his grin probably matched hers.

"Is this a real date?" she asked with her head tilted, her goofy grin still stretching her lips.

"Um...is there a reason it's supposed to be? I mean, we're watching kids, not exactly doing anything romantic."

"I was just wondering if I could expect a kiss at the end of the evening or not." She gave a little, almost playful shrug of her shoulders. "That way I know whether to be nervous or not."

His stomach had started swinging around in slow loops, and now it felt tight and hard.

He took a step closer and put a hand on the back of her neck, underneath her hair which was soft against his skin.

He ran his other hand down her arm and around the small of her back, pulling her closer. Her eyes widened and then darkened, and her lips parted.

"Maybe I should just kiss you now and get it over with." He grinned a little. "Is that what I should do? You know, do the worst first, so you can enjoy the rest of the evening? That's what you're saying, right?"

"No." She drew the word out, then gave her head a small shake. "Yes. That's exactly what I was saying. Do the worst first."

He felt his lips turning up as a smile he couldn't quite stop spread across his face.

He bent down, brushing his lips over her temple, feeling heady with the knowledge that she did indeed want him to kiss her.

He also liked the idea that she was nervous.

And he liked even more that her hands had come up and gone around his shoulders, and she was doing something to the back of his neck that he didn't care if she never stopped.

But it probably wasn't a good idea to have their first kiss on Mrs. Hudson's doorstep, with her front door hanging wide open, and six kids waiting on them to get there, as well as a bunch of men hoping to take Pastor Gus away.

"I don't think I have enough time to kiss you the way I want to. So I think we better wait."

"You just want to torture me."

"Busted. Is it torture?"

She nodded. "Pretty close."

"Good. I didn't want to be the only one feeling that."

"You're not. And I think it's sadistic that makes you feel better."

"Sadistic. And she still wants me to kiss her. I think I like you."

"I think it scares me that you do."

"I think I'm the one that should be scared. Falling for a woman who likes sadistic men."

She shook her head. "Don't make 'men' plural. Because it's not."

"Good. I'd be kind of upset if it were."

Her eyes were serious when she looked at him. Her smile had faded. "Me too."

"That's not something you have to worry about. I've got other faults."

"Nobody's expecting perfection."

"It's a good thing, because you're not getting it with me."

"I don't want it." Her look became sincere. "Because I'm not perfect. It would be terrible if someone as imperfect as I am got together with the perfect man. It makes me feel inferior just thinking about it."

Her thumb ran up the side of his neck, and he kind of forgot to breathe. Thankfully, he didn't lose the thread of the conversation.

"You're not inferior. I have the thought that I don't deserve you run through my head about a hundred times every hour. Not even sure what you are doing standing here with me."

"I'm wondering why you're determined to torture me all evening, and I'm hoping that you change your mind. That's what I'm doing."

"Remember? Sadistic."

"Remember? I don't care."

She felt warm and soft under his hands, and he wanted to just pull her close and hold her and forget about the kids and the men and the responsibilities that he had, just spend the evening holding her and talking to her, telling her about his dad and the company and the things he needed to do, and ask her if she'd be interested in doing any of that with him and, if not, if there was any chance of them being together if he stayed in Cowboy Crossing or followed her around the country wherever she went, which he'd do if there was even the slightest chance she'd take him.

He almost had to think there was. She wasn't the kind of woman who was going to stand on the porch and talk about kissing while she was holding him when she wasn't interested in at least some kind of relationship.

Maybe she wasn't thinking permanence, but he hoped with all his heart and soul that she was.

He could hardly wait to ask her. But he closed his mouth around the words.

When he talked about it, he wanted to have enough time to have a full conversation. He didn't want to rush, and have a misunderstanding, and not be able to talk it out.

And he was serious about the time it was going to take him to kiss her.

He didn't have nearly enough time.

"Do you need to say goodbye to Mrs. Hudson?"

"No. She's finishing up the pantry, and then I kind of think she might be spending a little time online." She gave Preston a grin that made his brows pull together.

"Online? Mrs. Hudson?"

Athena nodded. "I think it's serious."

"It?"

Athena nodded again. "I believe she has a budding romance, and she's going to spend some time online with him."

"Mrs. Hudson. A budding romance. And she's meeting the man online? Why doesn't she just go to the next farm over and talk to him there?"

Athena shook her head. "No. It's not him."

"You're kidding." He felt like the world had moved a little, since Mrs. Hudson seemed so steady. "Are you telling me she has a possible romance going on, and it's not a farmer?"

"That's exactly what I'm saying."

"Wow. I suppose the next thing you're going to say is somebody's walking on water."

"That hasn't happened yet." Athena gave him an eyeball. "But I wouldn't discount it."

Chapter Twenty

During the ride over Preston had coordinated with Deacon and the other men who were staging the intervention.

It didn't shock Athena when they caught up to Deacon's car on Pastor Gus's Lane and both vehicles arrived together.

"He might not be willing to come, and if not, we're going to make him," Deacon said, after they got out of their cars and met at the front walk.

Deacon's serious eyes settled on Athena. "I don't how this is going to go down, but, if we end up having to carry him out, I'd appreciate it if you could try to make sure the kids don't get hurt."

Athena blinked. She couldn't keep her eyelids from fluttering up and down.

Carry him out?

She couldn't imagine Pastor Gus struggling that much, but she nodded her head seriously, and tried not to look as shocked as she felt.

Deacon gave her a reassuring smile. "We're going to do everything we can to help him. It just might not look great at the beginning."

"It's fine. You guys do what you need to. I'll take care of the kids."

She'd never quite done anything like this before, and she wasn't feeling too sure about it, but she happened to catch Preston's eye as he glanced at her, and he gave her a smile.

She wasn't sure what exactly he might have been thinking, but she was thinking about their conversation about the kiss, and a shiver went up her backbone.

She thought she was able to hide it.

Deacon was saying something to Preston about helping her with the kids, unless they needed help with Pastor Gus, but it didn't really involve her and she kind of tuned him out, because she was thinking about the conversation Preston and she had just had.

She hadn't mentioned her fear about him going back to alcohol, and he hadn't mentioned it at all either.

She didn't know where she thought "they" were going, and he hadn't said anything about that either.

Basically all they'd agreed on was that they wanted to kiss each other.

Hardly a relationship.

This was where she needed to break it off if that's what she was going to do.

She couldn't just go around kissing guys that she wasn't planning on being long-term with.

And long term to her meant a ring.

She hadn't ever had a relationship for the sake of having a relationship.

Why not?

The voice in her head was insidious, but she pushed back. Hard.

She wasn't that kind of girl.

She wasn't going to be happy with anything less than the real deal. And she didn't want anything less than vows and a ring.

She'd always figured anything less was a waste of time.

What was the point of dating just for the sake of dating?

She supposed it was fine for some people, and that was fine with her, but it had never been something she'd even considered.

Maybe she would have had more relationships if she had.

She didn't exactly regret that at this point though. Dating and breaking up seemed an awful lot like practice for marriage and divorce.

If all a couple knew how to do when they couldn't get along anymore was breakup, they didn't exactly learn how to work through anything.

She had to admit, her views were a little eccentric compared to the rest the world. Preston probably didn't feel that way it all.

In fact, she knew he didn't.

After all, he had a son. Thinking about Liam, she looked over in time to see Preston finishing up a text and hitting "send."

He looked up and caught her eye.

"Liam?" she asked.

He nodded. "He's fine. In fact, he just texted me and asked if he could stay overnight."

"Are you letting him?"

"I told him I'd talk to Clark about it later." He shrugged. "I can't always let him do whatever he wants, but it feels like he just lost his mom, and if he's distracted by playing at a friend's house, I'll let him."

That made sense to her, and she didn't say anything, but just nodded.

They'd climbed up on the porch steps, and the other men had stepped back along with Preston and her, while Deacon knocked on the door. Athena assumed that they didn't want to go in there looking like a military brigade and put Pastor Gus on the defensive immediately.

There was a crash and a yell from inside. Deacon's fingers twitched.

The door opened. The yell become a scream which became louder as the door was pulled back, and Pastor Gus appeared.

Athena had to admit it had been a long time since she'd seen him, and she was a little shocked at his appearance.

His hair was so long it touched his shoulders, and his beard, streaked with gray, was down past the collar of his shirt.

His face looked haggard, and his eyes were bloodshot.

The T-shirt he wore might have been white at one time, but it was spotted with stains, old and new, on top of a greyish pink base color.

It looked like he was wearing a pair of woman's shorts. At least they were pink and kind of bell shaped, which gave the appearance that he wore a miniskirt.

Athena averted her eyes at the vast expanse of hairy leg that was exposed, although she did notice that he wore one sock. There was a hole at the end, and his little toe stuck out, looking for all the world like it had been sewed on or something.

She hadn't been too keen on the whole intervention thing, feeling like the man deserved to be able to grieve, and in his own way and for as long as he needed to.

The screaming hadn't stopped, and two kids ran by, one carrying a baseball bat.

She felt a whole lot better about the intervention, but a whole lot worse about actually having to watch those children.

She didn't figure she had to make a mental note about getting the baseball bat out of the kid's hands first thing.

Before anyone could say anything, there was a crash, and the sharp, tinkling sound of glass breaking and scattering everywhere.

"I'm sorry. I better go take care of that. You guys will have to come back some other time." Pastor Gus backed up a step, and Athena was pretty sure he was gonna shut the door in their faces.

She hadn't been able to get her mouth closed, but thankfully Deacon was a little faster, and put a foot forward to stop the door.

"Preston and Athena are going to watch your children until my wife gets back with Ivory. Then they'll be here to take over. And they'll call reinforcements if necessary." Deacon said that with a straight face, but for some reason Athena had to bite back a smile.

She kinda thought she and Preston might need reinforcements too. And the idea that they might being that there were only six kids was scary and awe-inspiring at the same time.

"I feel like I should have brought handcuffs," Preston leaned over and whispered in her ear.

She didn't snort, but she wanted to. She had been having the exact same feeling. Handcuffs and duct tape. And, unless she missed her guess, about three hundred dollars worth of groceries too.

She doubted Pastor Gus had been cooking much.

"What do you mean they're going to be watching my kids. Why?" Pastor Gus said to Deacon.

"Because you need some tough love, and we're here to give it to you," Deacon said, and jerked his head at the men standing behind them.

"I'm not going anywhere. You're wasting your time." Pastor Gus tried to run a hand through his hair, but it got caught on something pink. Athena was pretty sure it was gum.

She swallowed against the closing in the back of her throat and willed her stomach contents to stay down.

"You guys need to go." His voice was lethargic and lifeless. Athena wasn't sure how long it had been since his wife died, but this was definitely long overdue.

He was almost certainly depressed.

Another child's screams had joined the first, and she wanted to push past Pastor Gus and race into the house, protecting whoever was in there from the glass on the floor.

She wasn't even sure how old the children were. Hopefully they were old enough to know that they couldn't walk through glass barefoot.

There were some brushing sounds and some more tinkling, and she thought that someone might be sweeping the mess up.

It hurt her heart a little bit, both for the kids and for their father, but she still couldn't wait for Pastor Gus to get out the doorway so she could push in.

She wanted to command Deacon to just grab him and haul him out, but, maybe Deacon would want to put some clothes on him first.

At the very least, Deacon probably wished he had more clothes on.

To be honest, so did she. There just wasn't anything appealing about his skinny, white and hairy legs. Not a thing.

She looked up at the ceiling and tried to keep from tapping her toe.

She wasn't sure, but she thought Preston swallowed his snort beside her.

Tempted to lean over and say she figured his legs were probably just as skinny, white and hairy as Pastor Gus's, she didn't.

Somehow, the idea of seeing Preston's legs was slightly more appealing.

If she were being completely honest, she wasn't sure whether she would avert her eyes if that pink, short/skirt thing had a twin and Preston decided to model it for her.

She almost laughed. What in the world was she thinking? She did not want Preston wearing something like that. No matter whether she got to see his legs or not.

She also wasn't completely ignorant of the fact that if Preston were having the same thoughts about her legs, it might not be as funny.

Deacon had been telling Pastor Gus that either he was going to come willingly or they were going to take him.

Pastor Gus had barely gotten the "no" out of his mouth before Deacon and one of the other men grabbed each arm, while someone else grabbed his legs, and they hauled him out.

"We've got this," Preston said as they walked by, Pastor Gus struggling, but not making any noise.

Preston took one step and stopped with his foot right inside the door. He turned to look at her. "Are you up for this?"

"I'm not sure," she said just as honest and sincere as she could be.

"Me either." He threw a glance over his shoulder, as a car door slammed. "I thought they might put him in the trunk."

"You mean they didn't?" Athena asked, looking.

"No. They shoved him in the back."

When she looked back, he was grinning. "I'm a little bummed because I was thinking to myself how good you'd look in that pink thing he was wearing." His grin got a little wicked. "There were a lot of legs."

"Shut up." She put a hand on his chest and shoved him aside, walking in the door. Completely and totally pretending that she hadn't been thinking the exact same thing about his.

Chapter Twenty-One

Six kids is a lot of kids.

That statement wouldn't have seemed so profound even an hour before they walked into Pastor Gus's house, but it definitely seemed profound to Preston as he had all the little bodies seated at the table, all with plates and silverware in front of them, and tried to figure out what kid went with what name, and which names he was forgetting, since he could only remember three.

He kinda gave up. They answered when he said "boy" or "girl." Which was good, because that's pretty much all he could manage.

And it had been up to him to manage, since Athena had walked in, cleaned up the glass, put a bandage on a small cut one of the little ones had from the glass, and, after asking the children if they had eaten, and been given a loud chorus of "no's," she'd set to work trying to find enough edible food in the cupboards to put together for some semblance of a meal, and it had been all his responsibility to watch the children.

He was outmatched, outmaneuvered, and out-everythinged.

But, no one had died, and they were all sitting at the table.

"Would you say grace for us please?" Athena asked, looking

down the double rows of three tow heads each from her end of the table to his.

"Of course." At least the children all seemed to know what that was, because every single one of them had their little hands folded together, and their heads bowed.

He swallowed. It wasn't that he never talked to God. He just never did it out loud. And never in front of Athena.

He kinda felt like she would be judging him. But he wasn't going to put on airs, just to impress her. That would be wrong. If she was going to be with him, he wanted it to be for him. With warts and all.

There was no point trying to be better than he was and hope she fell in love with someone that he wasn't and end up disappointed if anything ever did come of their relationship.

He felt like that was being unselfish of him, because he could end up losing her. Who he was wasn't anywhere near close to who he wanted to be, and he could be that for a little bit anyway.

But that wasn't honest. He didn't have a whole lot of good qualities to his name, but honesty was thankfully one of them.

"Let's pray," he said, bowing his own head and not looking at Athena. "Lord God, thank you for the food. Please bless the hands that prepared it. Thank you for the children sitting here and for their father. Heal his heart, and give him grace and strength to raise these little ones for you. I ask in the name of Jesus, Amen."

He didn't lift his head right away, because he had to bite his tongue over asking God to send Pastor Gus a wife. That's what he needed. The idea of trying to take care of all these kids by oneself, the idea of trying to navigate life alone... More than any man should have to do alone.

He realized part of his trouble when Shane had died, and he'd fallen in with the bottle, was that he'd been lonely.

He hadn't even seen that until he almost prayed for Pastor Gus's loneliness.

He shook his thoughts away and raised his head. The kids had started chattering among themselves as soon as he said "amen," but Athena still looked at him.

He couldn't read the look on her face. Couldn't tell whether he'd done a good job, or not, or if she was even thinking about that.

He figured she wasn't.

She wouldn't care. Not about that.

He picked up the spoon in the mashed potatoes and put a small scoop on the plates he could reach, while she served peas and meat gravy to the plates she could.

They exchanged serving pots and finished serving the kids.

Maybe six kids wasn't too many.

Not if he had the right woman at the other end of the table.

Two hours later, when their reinforcements had texted them and said that they'd gotten through the tractor but Ivory's mom had some kind of pain in her stomach and needed to be taken to the emergency room, he'd actually texted back and said they were doing okay.

Because it was true.

He felt like what was happening around them was controlled chaos anyway.

It was wild and crazy and loud, but they were having fun.

He'd never played games with his family growing up, but Athena had all the children, plus him and herself, playing Blind Man's Bluff.

Somehow the kids really liked it when he was blindfolded and they were hiding from him, so he was "it" a lot.

Which was good, because they were very still while they were hiding, and quiet even, since if they moved, Athena made them sit out until the next round.

The kids loved it, and begged to play long after he was ready for bedtime, which was about six o'clock.

At eight, Athena insisted on giving everyone a bath, and he couldn't disagree with that. They needed it. They weren't completely filthy, but it looked like it been several days since they'd seen any type of water on their bodies.

A couple of them really didn't want to get in the water, and he was almost convinced that they really would melt if they touched it, but no one did, and they'd gotten their jammies on and he'd invented another game, which had been an accident, since he'd been sitting in the living room and - the living room, dining room and kitchen made a big circle - one of the kids had gone by. Preston happened to be holding a pillow from the couch as he sat on the edge of the recliner, and he'd smacked the kid's butt with it.

Pretty soon all six kids were making a loop around the rooms and he was expected to smack each butt with a pillow every time.

The Smack Their Butt With a Pillow Game, which he creatively called it, lasted for a good half an hour.

"Okay guys, it's nine-thirty. I'm pretty sure it's bedtime," Athena said, looking as tired as he felt.

"At least they should all sleep good tonight, with all that running around."

"Actually, I think it works the opposite way. They're so wound up, I don't think they're going to go to bed. Want to go see if you can dig up some books somewhere?"

"We have books," one of the older boys said.

Preston couldn't keep the name straight. Still.

He kinda thought maybe the older boys were goofing off with their names, because he was pretty sure they had switched their names, and they'd even called one of the girls Luke. He must look like he was pretty stinking gullible if the boys thought he was going to believe Pastor Gus had named one of his daughters Luke.

Yeah. Names were for some other time.

It was another half an hour before Athena decided that they'd had enough story time and were ready to go to bed.

Since the kids slept in three different rooms, they'd all hunkered down on the hall floor. Athena with two little ones in her lap, and the other four either lying down or leaning against the wall, with one of them tucked next to him.

It felt kind of cozy to be honest, and not necessarily a scene he'd ever pictured himself in. But, he couldn't say that he minded. In fact, he kinda liked it. Which surprised him.

Athena took the two little girls to their room, and said their prayers with them, and chatted with them a bit. He could hear her as he put the two smallest boys to bed. One of them still so little that he slept in a crib.

Preston suspected the kid could probably climb out of the crib, but if that's where he belonged, that's where he put him.

It didn't take long to say their prayers, and tuck them in, turning off the light before going to the older boys' room.

Less than ten minutes later he met Athena in the dark hallway.

"You think they're going to go to sleep?" he asked.

"I think so. The little ones are anyway. The older ones are still pretty worked up." She tilted her head and grinned at him. "I think they really liked your game."

"Total accident."

"An accident that worked."

He forgot it was his turn to talk. Her smile hit everything that he was feeling just perfectly, and while he wouldn't have said that he exactly wanted to have six kids right then and there, he had to say, "I don't think I'd mind doing this every night."

Her eyes opened wide, and her mouth hung down. Her brows lifted and she said, "Really?"

He nodded. "I mean, it was a lot of work, don't get me wrong, and I would want our kids to be a little better disciplined, and I'd want to know their names —"

"Our kids? Ours?"

He snapped his mouth closed.

"Did I say ours?"

She nodded. They stood there and looked at each other for what felt like a really long time.

"Is that crazy?" he finally asked, softly, the hope he felt coming out more than he wanted it to, along with his insecurity. Or maybe it was his disbelief that Athena might want this with him.

He couldn't deny he'd said "our kids," and he wasn't thinking about doing this with anyone else.

For sure.

Her eyes searched his, and she seemed to swallow.

He didn't see it as a good sign when she backed up a step. "Preston... I..."

The door opened, and a voice called out in a muted tone, "You guys still alive?"

And then in a slightly astonished tone, the voice said, " Did you actually get the kids to bed?"

"Come on," Preston said to her, "Let's talk to Blair, and then maybe you and I can go somewhere and talk about this. I guess we probably should."

She nodded.

Maybe he shouldn't have, but when he turned, he took her hand. He didn't really give her a choice about it, and he threaded his fingers with hers.

She allowed it, and his heart wanted to feel hope, but he couldn't allow that. The look on her face, and the tone in her voice just now told him, there was not much chance for hope.

He ground his jaw together, wishing there was something he could do, wishing he had more time, wishing he had never touched a single bottle, because he was pretty sure that was it. He couldn't make her any promises he wasn't sure he could keep.

"We sure did. They're in bed, and they haven't made a peep since we put them there," Preston said with confidence.

"It was just five minutes ago though," Athena said, and he gave her a goofy look, like "Why did you have to say that?"

"Because it's the truth," she said, returning his goofy look.

"Wow. I'm impressed. I thought we were going to have to use this," Blair said, holding up a roll of duct tape.

"And these," Marlowe said, holding up three sets of handcuffs.

"They came prepared," Preston said, duly impressed.

"We know for next time," Athena said, eyeing Preston.

"We're totally kidding. We just thought we'd mess with you guys. We figured you would mob us when you saw the duct tape and handcuffs. We had no idea you'd be so good at this." Marlowe gave Athena an impressed look. "I should have known. You're organized and you probably had them eating out of your hand."

"No. Definitely not that. Preston was really good at playing games with them, and I think they're just starved for attention. They snuggled and listened to stories for a really long time."

Marlowe's face fell a little and Blair looked serious as well. "We know. We probably should have done this earlier, but we were just hoping that Pastor Gus would snap out of it. They need their dad. Although, they do need affection, and they miss their mother as well."

Athena had to agree with that, and she nodded.

"You all good if we hit the road?" Preston asked.

"We're good. You guys did all the heavy work."

"I didn't get the dishes done," Athena said.

"Not a problem. We've got it."

They said their goodbyes, then Preston tugged on Athena's hand, and he followed her out when he opened the door for her.

After they'd stepped off the porch, he said, "How about we just walk here? If you don't mind?"

"That's fine," Athena said, and she fell into step beside him.

He saw that as a good thing, but maybe she was just eager to get this over with, so they could break off whatever it was that they had going between them and go their separate ways.

"I —"

"I —"

They started together, and then laughed.

"You go first," he said.

"No you. I want to hear what you have to say."

"Well, I want to hear what you have to say too, but I guess if you don't mind, I would like to go first."

"That's fine."

He wasn't sure how to begin. He supposed the best way was to just open his mouth and start saying the things he needed to say. He thought again of what he had been thinking as they sat at the table and she waited for him to pray.

He didn't want to be somebody he wasn't.

He didn't want her to fall in love with a man he'd made up, and pretended to be long enough to impress her, only to find out he wasn't what she thought.

That sounded like a good thought to start with.

How to say it?

"It's tempting to me to be fake, to pretend to be better than I am, because it's so important to me for you to think well of me, and for years I know you didn't. And rightfully so."

"It's not that I didn't. I was just so angry that you were wasting everything you had."

"You're right. I was wasting my life. "

"And you had so much potential." She shook her head. "Have. You *have* so much potential."

He took three more steps, biting his tongue and thinking about that one.

"Have?"

"Of course. You're brilliant. You always have been. But you're funny and you're fun and you're smart but you're not a stick in the mud. Your parents have a business, and you were helping them in it, doing great things. You could be a true example to other believers. If you were to get right."

"You're right about that. I guess. Deacon said there were lessons to be learned from Shane death. I thought he was crazy at first. I didn't see any lessons. But there are."

When he didn't go on, she prompted him. "What?"

He thought that was a good sign too. At least she was interested in what he had to say.

"Everything I do is a choice. Everything that's happened to me is my choice. I realized that I can choose to feel the pain of Shane death. I can choose to hear the scream. I can choose to hear it cut off. I can choose to replay that over and over in my head."

And he had. For years he had. Not even realizing it was a conscious choice.

But it had been.

He had chosen to waste his life that way. No more.

"Or I can choose to control my thoughts. I can choose to think about something else instead of drowning the screams out with alcohol. I can choose to replace those thoughts anytime my mind starts to go there with something else."

He looked over at her, curious as to what she was thinking, But her face didn't give anything away. She had one lip pulled in and looked down at the ground.

He felt like it was hopeless.

Sure, earlier she had wanted to kiss him. But now that she had time to think about it, she'd probably realized they were all wrong for each other.

He fell silent, all the things he'd wanted to say, didn't seem to be enough.

Chapter Twenty-Two

Athena tried to remember all of the arguments she had against being with Preston.

Why was she so tempted to forget them?

Tempted to throw away her common sense and everything she knew to be right, and just take a risk.

Thankfully, before she could say anything, he started speaking again.

"I thought about trying to be somebody I'm not. Somebody better. When you'd asked me to pray, I've been in church enough I could pray a really good prayer. It would sound authentic, and I think I could have fooled you. But...that's not really where I am with the Lord right now, and even though I think that was another lesson that I needed to learn — that God is in control, and no one lives or dies without God's sovereignty orchestrating everything — I didn't think it was right."

"Really? You learned that?"

"Of course." He nodded, and something fluttered in the area of her heart. "My life, the risks I've taken, there's no reason I should have survived. I questioned for a long time why I did and Shane didn't. But, if God has the very hairs on our head numbered, he's got our breaths numbered too. And nothing I can do will change that. Even suicide. God has to allow it. How many foiled suicide attempts have there been?"

"I don't want to think about that."

"That's just it. Sometimes we have to think about the hard things. Face them. Walk through them. With our eyes open, looking around and learning what we're supposed to."

"Face your fear."

"Yeah. Just like that. As soon as Deacon said to start looking for the lessons, they showed up everywhere. Up until Shane died, I had thought I was invincible. We all did. I came face-to-face with my own mortality, and realized in just a couple of seconds, it could have been me." He let out a shaky breath.

She wanted to put her arms around him.

"Talk about a long climb down off the wall."

"I bet. Long and hard. For a lot of different reasons."

"You're telling me. Because of what we knew was at the bottom. Because of what we'd just witnessed. Because of what we'd just realized about ourselves."

"I think you're right. You have really put some thought into that."

"Deacon raked me over the coals; he forced me to open my eyes, and face my stupidity. I already had decided to quit drinking because of Liam, but I don't know if I could have stuck with it, because the pain hadn't gone away. It got worse when I gave up the bottle."

"I see. There was a choice to stop drinking, and then there was Deacon showing you how to handle it without the alcohol."

"Yeah. Without that, I might not have made it. I still might not."

She felt like he was being as honest as he could be with her. Almost brutally so. He hadn't had to say that.

She stopped. He turned to face her.

"I can't pretend anything else," he said.

"I appreciate it." The fluttering had gotten stronger, and she thought it might be hope.

But it might be fear too. Because she needed to take a risk.

"It's kind of ironic, that you quit taking risks, and I feel like maybe I'm about to take one myself."

His eyes flinched, and she wasn't sure exactly what that meant.

"In what way?" he asked, cautiously.

"I still want to kiss you."

Talk about taking risks. That had been hard. She had no idea how he felt. He might have been warning her away because he'd decided he didn't want her.

"I haven't changed my mind either."

That was a relief. But she had to do more. He wasn't going to pretend to be anything he wasn't, and she had to be honest as well.

"I don't go around kissing just anyone."

"I didn't think you did."

"I don't want just kissing."

Long seconds ticked by, while he seemed to process the implications of what she said. She had no idea where his mind was going, so she added some more.

"I guess I've never felt you should walk into a relationship thinking anything less than it's a serious thing, with long-term implications. I don't play relationship games."

"I know. I don't want to anymore. I did a lot of stupid things, and stupid things typically do nothing but leave big regrets."

She nodded. She'd done her share of stupid things, but not on the relationship side.

At least not yet.

She wasn't getting the feeling that this was a stupid thing. She did think she was taking a risk, but maybe it was how he had talked about the Lord, and the decisions that he made that had given her the feeling that everything was going to be okay.

Preston seemed like less of a risk and more of a sure thing.

Also, he'd been so good with the kids tonight. Watching him had been beautiful because he was so gentle and kind, yet rough enough to mark a sharp difference between himself and her.

She liked their differences.

"I think you might be asking me to marry you. And I haven't even kissed you yet," he finally said.

"Is there something wrong with that?" she asked, feeling brave.

"I guess not. I actually kind of like that. We could have our first kiss as man and wife."

Maybe her bottom lip stuck out a little bit, she wasn't sure. She hadn't been thinking along those lines, although there was a certain appeal there. But she'd had her heart set on tonight.

"I suppose we could."

"You don't sound excited about that."

"I'm more excited about having it tonight."

That made him smile, a confident smile, as he looked at her with tenderness in his eyes.

Which made her feel safe.

"I think that's something we're in agreement on."

"Kissing tonight?" she asked, the hope in her tone making his smile grow even bigger.

"Yeah. But first, maybe I should tell you that I want to marry you. That's where this is going. And, you know I come with a kid and, we haven't even talked about what were going to do."

"Do?"

"My parents want me to go to Houston and work in the business. But we thought we could stay here in Cowboy Crossing, or I could follow you around the country from job to job, and work remotely with whatever dad gives me."

"They want you in Houston? For something specific?"

"A leadership position has opened up, and dad said I'd worked for it, which is true. Before Shane died, I had put a lot of time in the company. Since I was about twelve."

"I know. Your dad had you there all the time."

"Yeah, except when I was with Andrew and Shane."

"You loved it."

"I did. But...I guess you might as well know, I love you more."

She gasped. She couldn't help it. She supposed they were talking about kissing and relationships and, marriage even, and it shouldn't have surprised her, but she knew immediately that she could return those words.

Maybe he needed to hear them.

"I want you to know, I admire what you've done in the short time that you've been here, taking Liam, having Joyce in your home, quitting the alcohol, and coming to terms with Shane... All of it. When you decided to get right, you didn't mess around." She smiled. "I love you too. I have for a long time."

He seemed surprised at that. "How long?"

She laughed, a little self-consciously. "Before we graduated. I don't know. How long have you and Andrew been friends?"

"You're kidding." He shook his head, his mouth open in disbelief. "You were so serious. So different. I had no idea."

"I know. I didn't think you could ever fall for someone like me."

"You're the kind of person that complements me perfectly. You are exactly what I need."

She couldn't argue with that. She happened to agree.

"And I need you. I need you to push me out of where I'm comfortable and make me take risks."

"Hmm." He stepped closer, sliding his hand behind her back, and folding their hands that were clasped together between them. "So, is it too far out of your comfort zone to kiss a man in the moonlight?"

"Not as long as it's you."

"I think I'd be kind of upset if you were kissing someone else."

"I can't imagine that I would want to." Athena shuddered. It was true. Kinda funny if she thought about it, but she didn't, because she stepped closer until they were touching, and lifted her free hand up to his neck.

His eyes seem to search her face, maybe checking and making sure that she really wanted this, before his head lowered, and he kissed her, soft and sweet, and she sighed, a whisper across his lips, before it became something different, and she liked that too.

She wasn't sure how long it was before he finally lifted his head, and rested his cheek against hers, and whispered in her ear, "I want more."

She didn't say anything. He could probably feel her trembling, and she wasn't sure she could form words.

Maybe waiting for years to kiss a man had that effect on everyone, but she hadn't been expecting it.

"So much better than I imagined," she whispered, her cheek still against his, her heart erratic in her chest.

"I didn't know I had a standard to live up to," he said, and there was a tremble in his voice too.

"Maybe I've imagined this a time or two." Maybe she shouldn't admit that.

"I can admit that I have too, but when I imagined it, you never weakened my knees and took my breath away. It was always me doing that to you."

"I guess we did it to each other."

"I'm fine with that."

"Me too. I look forward to more."

"I hope you don't make me wait too long."

"Because of Liam?"

He laughed a little. "It would be nice to have a stable home for him. But I don't want to rush you into anything." He lifted his head back, and took a deep breath, as though steadying himself. "I don't have a ring and I don't have a fancy anything prepared, and you deserve it all, but...would you marry me?" he asked, and he sounded so unsure, like after everything they'd talked about, she still might turn him down.

"Yes." She wasn't going to string him along, or make him wait.

"How long will it take you to plan the wedding?"

"We can get married tomorrow."

He tilted his head to the side. It was a little too dark for her to see his face, but his voice sounded like it was full of disbelief. "Surely you want a wedding with all the trimmings - white dress, flowers and bridesmaids and whatever else people have." He waved a hand, then slid it back around her waist. "I know that doesn't happen overnight."

"I think we'll be just as married if I wear what I'm wearing now, and we do it tomorrow without all that. I think I would keep my sanity, and so would you, and so would everyone around us, that would probably be a good thing, too." Her fingers twisted the hair at the nape of his neck. She liked the way it curled around her fingers.

"Maybe we should wait a week."

"Maybe we should. I'll have a new assignment, unless..." She thought about what she was saying, and immediately she knew it was what she wanted. "If you want to go to Houston. I won't have any trouble finding a job there. In a hospital, as a home nurse, even with hospice again. There are jobs everywhere. I can get one wherever we go."

"I kinda like it here in Cowboy Crossing."

"Then let's stay."

"Let's see what Liam says. Is that okay with you?"

"It's fine with me. There aren't any hospitals nearby, but there's an acute care center, and a couple of doctors' offices. I can find something wherever we go. You and Liam can decide."

"Are you sure about that?"

"Completely sure." And she was. Her job was the one that would be the easiest to move around, and Liam needed to be their focus. It felt right and good and she was sure it was the best thing.

"Have I mentioned lately that I love you?" he asked softly, bending his head again.

"I don't think so."

"I love you, lady."

Epilogue

"You have a wife and a son?" Preston's mother asked with her brows lowered and that look that he had come to dread as a child.

"I know. It all happened kinda fast." He felt like a little kid again being called on the carpet.

"Mrs. Harding," Athena said, holding out her hand. "I don't know if you remember me from my teen years, but I believe I met you several times, and I spent a lot of time around your son. He was a good kid."

Preston's stomach squeezed. His mother could be so difficult to deal with, and he was not going to subject his son nor his wife to her fits of temper and her emotional manipulation.

But, to his surprise, his mother smiled.

"I remember you. Athena. You are the only girl I could ever see my son with, the only girl I thought could handle him. He's met his equal in you." His mother, regal, held out her own beringed hand, her bracelets jangling, as she shook Athena's.

Someone else might have hugged her. But that wasn't really his mother.

Then she looked over at Liam. He stood, looking somewhat scared, beside Athena.

She had her arm around him, loosely, and he pressed into her side.

"And this is your child?" his mother asked Preston.

"He is."

"And he's yours too?" His mother asked, looking at Athena.

Athena didn't hesitate. "He is."

Preston felt warm all over, in a good and beautiful way.

Liam gave half a smile, and looked at Athena like he couldn't believe that she would claim him.

But there was also some hesitation in Liam's eyes, and Preston figured this was his story to explain.

He should have done it to begin with.

"Liam's mother passed away not long ago from an inoperable brain tumor. Liam is as much Athena's as he is mine."

"As much as he wants to be," Athena agreed, smiling benevolently at Liam, who grinned up at her, although his eyes held shadows, as though Preston talking about his mother had darkened his day.

Preston hated that he had to do that, but he wanted to be clear with his mom, and not put Liam on the spot.

Athena had handled it beautifully, the only way she really could have and Liam seemed open to the idea, but they didn't need to rush anything.

Athena would agree with that.

Maybe the years had softened his mother, because she held her hand out to Liam, before stepping forward and changing her mind, wrapping her arm around him. Even though she didn't really pull in close, it was a hug at least. Which was more than his mother typically gave.

"My goodness, Mitch. Can you believe this? A grandchild. And we didn't even have any idea."

His dad grunted. "I can see the boy takes after you. He's got your eyes. And that stubborn chin. I hope he's got a sensible head on his shoulders. We can get him started learning the ropes of the business right away."

"If he wants to," Athena said, inserting herself without being rude, but letting his parents know that they weren't going to bypass her and dictate what happened in Liam's life.

Preston tried to hide his smile. He felt like his mother had said he'd met his match, but he also felt like Athena would match his mother, without fighting with her.

He'd been blessed.

"So, you're staying in Houston?" his dad asked.

"Yes. For now. We'll be looking for property with a small amount of acreage around Cowboy Crossing. We'll have a second home there. With plans to eventually base our family there. But for now, we'll be here, in Houston."

His dad nodded. "We can work with that. Thank you."

"I need to thank you, Dad. Thank you for not giving up on me. Thank you for giving me this chance."

"You're my son. I'm proud of you."

That made his heart happy. It made it even happier to see Athena smile and glow, for him.

His dad held out his hand. "Welcome back son."

———

Join Jessie's list and be the first to know about new releases and sales on her books!

A Gift from Jessie

View this code through your smart phone camera to be taken to a page where you can download a FREE ebook when you sign up to get updates from Jessie Gussman! Find out why people say, "Jessie's is the only newsletter I open and read" and "You make my day brighter. Love, love, love reading your newsletters. I don't know where you find time to write books. You are so busy living life. A true blessing." and "I know from now on that I can't be drinking my morning coffee while reading your newsletter – I laughed so hard I sprayed it out all over the table!"

Claim your free book from Jessie!

Escape to more faith-filled romance series by Jessie Gussman!

The Complete Sweet Water, North Dakota Reading Order:

Series One: Sweet Water Ranch Western Cowboy Romance (11 book series)

Series Two: Coming Home to North Dakota (12 book series)

Series Three: Flyboys of Sweet Briar Ranch in North Dakota (13 book series)

Series Four: Sweet View Ranch Western Cowboy Romance (10 book series)

Spinoffs and More! Additional Series You'll Love:

Jessie's First Series: Sweet Haven Farm (4 book series)

Small-Town Romance: The Baxter Boys (5 book series)

Bad-Boy Sweet Romance: Richmond Rebels Sweet Romance (3 book series)

Sweet Water Spinoff: Cowboy Crossing (9 book series)

Small Town Romantic Comedy: Good Grief, Idaho (5 book series)

True Stories from Jessie's Farm: Stories from Jessie Gussman's Newsletter (3 book series)

Reader-Favorite! Sweet Beach Romance: Blueberry Beach (8 book series)

Blueberry Beach Spinoff: Strawberry Sands (10 book series)

From Strawberry Sands to: Raspberry Ridge (12 book series)

Swoonfully Jolly Holiday Stories:

Holiday Romance: Cowboy Mountain Christmas (6 book series)

Cowboy Mountain Christmas Spinoff: A Heartland Cowboy Christmas (9 book series)

New and Much Loved: Mistletoe Meadows (4 books and counting!)

Laughing Through the Snow: Christmas Tree, PA Sweet Romcoms (6 short reads)